Search Behind the Lines

Yevgeny Ryss
SEARCH BEHIND
THE LINES

Translation from the Russian by Bonnie Carey
William Morrow and Company • New York 1974

Library of Congress Cataloging in Publication Data

Ryss, Evgeniĭ Samoĭlovich.
    Search behind the lines.

    SUMMARY: Two children face the perils of the German oc-
cupation of Russia during World War II.
    Translation of Devochka ishchet ottsha.
    1. Russia—History—German occupation, 1941–1944— Juvenile
fiction. [1. Russia—History—German occupation, 1941–1944—
Fiction] I. Title.
PZ7.R987Se   [Fic]   74-6553
ISBN 0-688-21831-8
ISBN 0-688-31831-2 (lib. bdg.)

Translator's Note

There is an old Russian proverb which states that "a good product is its own praise." Certainly it is true of good stories. Kolya's and Lena's adventures in war-ravaged Soviet Russia during Nazi occupation need no embellishment.

An explanation of how Yevgeny Ryss's novel happened to be translated from Russian into English is more in order, for few people in the United States have heard the author's name. As translator, I must admit that my initial contact with the story was purely accidental. Translators continually read foreign books in hopes of finding stories they consider worthy of being put into English. Consequently, I came across *Search Behind the Lines*.

Spellbound, I read the book from cover to cover in one sitting. It was clear to me that young people would enjoy meeting Kolya and Lena and the other Russian children in the story, that they would grow as fond of them as I. From that time on, accident no longer played a role in the translation of the novel. Work and determination, ingredients for all translations, took over. I began translating each Russian word of the novel into its English equivalent, writing and rewriting until the story read smoothly.

I sent a letter to Yevgeny Ryss's editor, who very efficiently forwarded my communication to the author. In the fall of 1971, his answer arrived just as I was preparing to leave on a trip to Moscow. There was no time to reply, so I resolved to visit the author at his Moscow home.

The Soviet capital with its golden cupolas, muted autumn colors, and fairy tale Kremlin was unforgettable, but efforts to contact Ryss were futile. An Intourist guide, sympathetic but endowed with a determination equal to mine, insisted that it would be impossible to visit the author, who was gravely ill.

The illness that prevented our meeting that autumn loomed forebodingly over all our subsequent correspondence. Upon returning home from the Soviet Union, I sent the author several chapters I had been working on and asked for his opinion and good wishes. He generously granted both, but his reply took months in arriving. Because his illness had become more serious, he wrote from his hospital bed, "I am letting you know, although belatedly, that I am completely satisfied with the sample chapters that have been translated. I have been promised that I may leave the hospital around the beginning of June and, after spending a few days at home, go away with my wife to rest for a month or two. I will probably be home in September. It would be very nice to receive news about the translation from you at that time. If the publishing house wishes, I can write a brief preface for the American reader."

At the appropriate time, I informed Yevgeny Ryss of the translation's progress, assuring him that his preface would be a most welcome addition. I also asked for his help with the rendition of a few difficult passages that required knowledge of Soviet dialects and colloquialisms.

Once again his answer was slow to arrive. Excusing himself for the tardiness of his reply, which had been caused by his illness, he explained in precise Russian the meaning of the troublesome passages and promised to send the preface whenever it was needed.

The preface, obviously partially composed and perhaps even completed, never arrived. That was the last letter I received from him. In September of

1973, I wrote with great excitement to tell him that William Morrow and Company wanted to publish his story. His wife, Ludmila Ryss, wrote in reply that her husband, Yevgeny Samoilovich Ryss, had died on April 28 of that year.

The haunting illness had severed the ties of our friendship, which had been so tenuously balanced across great distances of space and differing cultural backgrounds. It is with sorrow and a feeling of humility that I have undertaken to write in his place the preface to his novel.

What sort of man was Yevgeny Ryss? He was kind, patient, and unprejudiced. He took time, when little remained, to help a translator whom he didn't know from a country which until recently had been considered an enemy of his own. He was a man who loved young people, who understood them, and who could spin a tale to captivate the young at heart. He was my friend. After you have read his novel, he will be your friend, too.

Yevgeny Ryss was born in 1908 and published his first book when he was twenty years old. He worked for some time for a newspaper. When World War II broke out, he became a war correspondent. A number of his plays (most of them for children) have been produced, and according to the author he has written "more than ten books." *Search Behind the Lines,* first published in 1946, was made into a prize-winning Russian movie.

It is unfortunate that Yevgeny Ryss will never have the pleasure of seeing the English version of his story. I offer the translation to you, the reader, in his memory. Travel with me to Byelorussia. Run with Kolya and Lena from the dreadful Nazis. Hide with them in a little village, and perhaps, like me, you will want to return to visit those brave people who suffered through a cruel war with courageous endurance and indomitable spirit.

Bonnie Carey
Raleigh, North Carolina
January, 1974

Contents

Search Behind the Lines

Dear Readers:

This is the story of Lena, the daughter of a famous Soviet general, who was left all alone in a country occupied by Hitler's army during World War II.

I know many true stories about how the Germans tried to capture wives, parents, or children of Soviet soldiers.

The details of Lena Rogachova's adventures are imaginary. I don't know the real name of her adopted cousin or the last names of either the teacher who hid her or the man who cured her of a serious illness. And there was no General Rogachov in the Soviet Army at the time.

Yet this story is based on the truth. Risking their own lives, the Russian people saved the wives, parents, and children of soldiers and officers who were fighting the Nazis.

Yevgeny Ryss

1

The Solomin Family Grows

An old schoolteacher by the name of Ivan Ignatye-vich Solomin lived with his grandson, Kolya, in the quiet little town of Zapolsk in Byelorussia. They lived all by themselves in a small wooden house. The boy's parents had died when he was very young. Ivan Ignatyevich also had a daughter named Valya, who was Kolya's aunt. But she lived in Moscow and hadn't been able to get home to visit her father for many years.

Solomin was sixty-three years old, and Kolya was nine. Every morning the two of them set out for school together—Ivan Ignatyevich to teach, and his grandson to learn. When they returned home from school, they prepared dinner together. After dinner they chatted for a while and told each other the news. The little boy talked about his class, and the old man talked about his pupils. Then Kolya worked on his lessons for the next day as Ivan Ignatyevich corrected his students' notebooks. Sometimes Kolya went to the movies or the skating rink in the evening, and Solomin either read a book or visited his friend, Doctor Krechetov, for a game of chess. Afterward they talked over everything that had happened during the day, then went to bed. The little boy went first. The old man soon followed.

When Valya sent letters from Moscow, the old schoolteacher joyfully read them to his little grandson. Every spring Valya wrote, "Lena and I will try to visit you this summer without fail. You'll finally get to see your little granddaughter, and Kolya will meet his cousin."

Ivan Ignatyevich Solomin had inherited a little cottage, which was located in the remote depths of a forest, from his father. It was about fifty kilometers from Zapolsk and ten kilometers from the nearest village.

The old man's father had been a forester. He had loved the forest more than anything in life. After his death, the little cottage stood boarded up. Ivan Ignatyevich and Kolya always intended to go there in the summertime. They had to collect the things his old father had kept in the country. Besides they were eager to take a vacation in the forest for a while. But every year they put off the trip on account of Valya. Each summer they thought would certainly be the one she would come with little Lena.

They waited in vain. In autumn, Valya always sent a letter informing them that she couldn't make the trip, but would be sure to come next summer.

Finally they stopped waiting. When the school year ended in 1941, Kolya went to a Young Pioneer camp. Ivan Ignatyevich was all alone and missed his little grandson.

"Rent out a room for the summer," his friend, Doctor Krechetov, advised him. "Then you'll be with other people, and you won't be so lonely."

"And you'll make enough money to have a new coat sewed for Kolya," added Avdotya Timofeyevna, the lady who lived next door.

Solomin thought the advice over and stuck up a notice, which stated that he had a room for rent. He posted the notice in the morning. That evening a soldier came with his wife and a little blond girl.

"I am Lena," said the little girl, offering the old schoolteacher her hand.

The soldier laughed. "I'm Colonel Rogachov," he said. "My unit is stationed a short distance from town. This is my wife and daughter, who have come from Moscow to spend the summer. They want to be closer to me."

They moved in with their things that very same day. The colonel went off to join his unit the next morning, and his wife and daughter stayed with Ivan Ignatyevich.

The old man soon became attached to the little girl. She was an affectionate, merry child. It seemed as if his own granddaughter, whom he had never seen, had finally come from Moscow to visit him. Her name was the very same as his granddaughter's, and she was even the exact same age—four years old. Moreover, judging from the letters Valya sent, his own Lena was blond, too, with a similar little turned-up nose.

Lena Rogachova played in the garden day after day. When it got dark, she would sit on Solomin's knee and stay there until she fell asleep. She called him Grandfather. He told her interesting stories and promised to take her to school with him to study.

One morning the little girl was awakened by loud bombing attacks, which sounded nearby. Her mother wasn't in the room. She called to her, but her mother didn't answer. Lena got scared. She was just about to cry and had already opened her mouth wide when there was such a sudden, loud explosion she forgot all about her tears. Glass began to shatter, and a piece of plaster fell out of the ceiling. Planes zoomed over the roof with a roar.

The sound of their engines faded into the distance. People ran down the streets screaming and shouting to one another. Then it was quiet. Lena crawled out of bed and stood up, trying to decide whether she should cry or simply open the door to go look for her mother. At that very moment Grandfather entered the room.

When Lena saw him, she asked, "Where's Mama?"

"You must get dressed, my little one," answered Ivan Ignatyevich. "We have to go. Mama is waiting for us."

He began to dress her hurriedly. He took a long time to find her stockings and nearly put her dress on inside out. Lena laughed and turned her dress to the right side.

Grandfather was in a big hurry. His hands were shaking. But finally, she was dressed. They went out onto the street.

"Where is Mama?" she asked again.

"Let's go! Let's go!" the old man repeated. "We must hurry."

He couldn't bring himself to tell the little girl her

mother had been killed by one of the first bombs
that fell on the town.

They ran down the entire length of the street and
went into the forest, which began abruptly behind
the last houses. There were many people in the
forest. Old men trudged along with walking canes.
Entire families walked together. Parents led little
children by the hand or carried them on their
backs. Some people were crying, others were silent,
and still others were talking with one another.
Several just sat by the wayside and watched the
people passing by.

An elderly man with rags wound around his leg
lay under a tree. A little girl about twelve years old
was sitting beside him, sobbing and wiping her
eyes with her fist.

Lena stopped Solomin to ask why the man was
lying there, why the girl was crying, and where her
own mother was. The old man didn't answer. He
just hurried the child along, saying they were going
to join her mother so she must walk as fast as possible and not keep her waiting.

It was sixty kilometers to the camp where Kolya
was staying. They walked all day long and spent
the night in the forest with strangers. The old man's
legs ached. He breathed heavily, and his heart felt

fluttery. He had to carry Lena on his back frequently.

After another day and night had gone by, Lena stopped being amazed at everything and decided it was normal for people to walk through the forest, spend the night by a campfire or simply under a tree, eat berries, have a drink of milk now and then, and suck on a crust of bread as though it were a delicacy.

Only after three days had passed did they reach Kolya's camp. The children were already gone. German patrols were walking down the roads, questioning the passersby in poor Russian about who they were and where they were going.

Solomin explained that he was a sick old man who had gone into the forest to escape the bombing and was now returning home. He told them the little girl was his granddaughter. Calling Lena his granddaughter was safer than telling the truth, for people said Hitler's troops were especially cruel to the families of Soviet soldiers.

The poor child has no mother, thought the old man. There's no way of knowing where her father is or even whether or not he's alive. She might as well be my granddaughter.

They didn't find Kolya right away. At last he

turned up in the neighboring village, where some kind people had given him shelter.

Kolya laughed and cried at the same time when he saw his grandfather. The old man sobbed with happiness, too. They kissed one another. Then Ivan Ignatyevich raised Lena in his arms. "Here is your new cousin," he said.

"Lena?" asked Kolya in surprise. "They finally came! And where is your mama, Lena?"

Solomin frowned a warning. The little boy became silent. He already knew from experiences of the last three days how people can perish in time of war.

The old man had called Lena Kolya's cousin, meaning only that from then on they both would grow up together as brother and sister. But the boy took him at his word and decided that the little blond girl was the daughter of Aunt Valya, that very aunt who had long been promising to visit them. At first this misunderstanding troubled Solomin. He wanted to explain Kolya's mistake to him, but finally decided that perhaps it would be better for the boy to consider Lena his real cousin. So, looking at the little girl, he kept silent.

At night all three of them settled down to sleep in a hayloft. Lena fell asleep quickly. Ivan Ignatyevich and Kolya began to decide what to do next. They didn't even want to think of returning to Zapolsk.

The grandfather and grandson talked together for a long while. It was quiet all around. A cricket was chirping monotonously. Somewhere a dog was rattling its chain, and a cow moved about in the barn now and then. If it wasn't for the distant glow of fire, they could have imagined that there was no war.

"You know what, Kolya," the old man finally said, "let's go to our cottage in the forest! We'll set out early tomorrow morning. It isn't far from here. We'll reach the village by evening, where we'll spend the night, and be there the day after tomorrow. I don't think anything could happen to us there. It's a remote, deserted place. I doubt that Hitler's soldiers will ever go that far into the country. We'll live there for a while. After the Nazis have been driven away, we'll return to town."

Kolya agreed to these plans right away.

Their little home in the forest was some distance from the road. Grass had grown over and covered the little path that led to it long ago. Solomin himself almost lost his way, so it was highly unlikely that somebody who had never been there before would be able to reach it.

The new inhabitants took a look at their possessions first of all. The cottage was in excellent condition. No one had been there since the death of Solomin's father. The tables, benches, beds, and stools required only minor repairs.

In the cupboard there were four cups, two knives, and three spoons. On the stove were three different sizes of cast-iron pots. The number of dishes they found was more or less sufficient, and the number and condition of the tools was even better.

The old schoolteacher's father had been a thrifty man. There were two plain saws, a bow saw, a woodchopper, two axes, three scythes, whetstones for sharpening scythes, files for sharpening the saws, tool kits, and a fairly good supply of nails. All this equipment was carefully laid out and only very slightly damaged.

One of the two buckets they found was rusted through. The other, however, was made of galvanized iron and was still in one piece. There were three wooden tubs in the cellar. They were cracked, but after being dunked in the lake for several days they swelled and stopped leaking when filled with water.

The next day Ivan Ignatyevich Solomin went to the village to collect his father's personal belongings, which were being kept by an old man they knew. Among them were many useful things—a holiday dress that had belonged to his mother, some old boots that were still in good condition (apparently they had been worn only on festive occasions), bed linen, about five shirts, two blankets, and a large supply of needles and thread. Solomin was happiest to find two warm sheepskin coats and two pairs of felt boots.

The old man couldn't carry everything back at the same time, so he had to make several trips. A whole week went by before everything was transported. Then they unpacked all the bundles and put the things in their proper places.

As they were working, it got dark. They boiled some water over a small fire, which they started with shavings of wood. After drinking the hot water, they put Lena to bed. She fell asleep right away.

Ivan Ignatyevich and Kolya went outside and sat down on the little porch. The trees were motionless, and the silvery lake was sparkling below them. From the hill on which the little cottage stood they could see the endless forest, which stretched out for many kilometers. Neither villages, nor houses, nor campfire smoke was visible. There were only fir trees, birches, and lakes. The absence of other people was both frightening and reassuring.

"Never mind," Ivan Ignatyevich said. "We'll live through this somehow. Our own soldiers will return soon. I'm certain of it."

2

A Forest Home

It turned out to be very difficult for them at first. They lived on a diet of fish, mushrooms, and berries. Fortunately, the fish bit as soon as a hook hit the water. And there were so many wild strawberries, raspberries, and bilberries that even Lena could pick a big basketful with little effort. They could gather a bucket of mushrooms just outside the cottage itself. Yet they couldn't live without bread and salt. Solomin had brought a small supply back from the village, but it was soon gone.

The first few times Ivan Ignatyevich had to go to the village, Lena felt bored without the old man, to whom she had become very attached. But Kolya found the absence of his grandfather not only dull, but terrifying. At night, while Lena was sleeping, Kolya often stayed awake for hours. The moon peeked into the windows, and tree branches rustled. Who was to say whether the rustling noise was a tree or a stranger? Maybe wild animals, such as wolves or bears, were outside. Maybe an enormous wolf would come out of the forest, raise its bloody snout to the moon, and howl. It was horrifying! Mice scrambled about under the floor, and the floorboards creaked from time to time. Kolya usually fell asleep only toward dawn.

Ivan Ignatyevich would come home from the village with salt and flour. One time he even bought some rye to plant. Gradually they became adjusted to life at their forest home.

One day at sunset, after Kolya and his grandfather had finished sawing wood, Kolya left the saw in the clearing in front of the cottage. He didn't notice its absence until it was already dark. Someone had to go get the saw, because it would rust if it were left out all night in the dew. Kolya didn't want to leave the cottage, but he was ashamed to admit it to his grandfather. So he went anyway.

The shadows of trees waved in front of him, taking on strange forms and moving constantly. They were frightening. The saw, as luck would have it, was lost somewhere out there. When Kolya finally found it and started back to the cottage, he heard the sudden, unmistakable sound of heavy breathing. He stopped and stood motionless—frozen with fear.

He distinctly heard footsteps. Grass and dry leaves

were crunching under somebody's feet. Kolya forced himself to turn around. Outlined by the wavering light of the moon, an animal was standing in the clearing—perhaps an enormous wolf, perhaps something even more terrible. Kolya ran into the cottage and, unable to utter a word, just gasped for breath and pointed at the door.

Solomin grabbed an ax and jumped up. Within a minute he called to Kolya laughingly. Beside the porch was a brown cow with white spots. She looked at Kolya with her gentle, dumb eyes.

Apparently the cow had come from someplace far away, from a village destroyed by the Nazis. Even if her owners were still alive, they could not find them. Without someone to take care of her, the cow would die. So Ivan Ignatyevich decided to keep her.

There was more and more work every day. They had to sharpen the scythes and do the mowing so that the cow would have enough hay for winter. Learning to milk was no simple matter either. But they always had fresh milk, cottage cheese, and sour milk on hand. In the fall, they dug up a strip of land and sowed the rye Solomin had bought.

That winter the old schoolteacher made a few more trips to the village.

Kolya and Ivan Ignatyevich were busy for days

on end. They cut and split wood, gave the cow hay, gathered manure to fertilize the rye, and went to the lake to icefish every day. Kolya learned to be a fairly good carpenter. He made a good sled, almost completely without his grandfather's help, and repaired many things in the cottage. One of the sheepskin coats ripped, and they made Lena a coat from what was left of it. Lena stayed outdoors a lot, sledding and building snowmen. She wasn't sick even once all winter long.

It got dark early. By the time they sat down to eat after having finished their daily work, it was already dusk. After their meal, they would light a pine splinter, which served as a kind of wooden candle to light the room. It would be warm—almost hot—in the little cottage. Lena would climb into bed and play quietly with a rag doll, getting her ready for bed or feeding her or telling her one of Grandfather's stories. Ivan Ignatyevich and Kolya would straighten up the cottage a bit. Afterward they sewed or mended. It was then that "night school" was held.

Solomin was the teacher, and Kolya was the student. Lena was simply a curious listener. Ivan Ignatyevich talked about countries in the north and south, about the journeys of Stanley and Livingston, and about the discoveries of the North and South Poles.

Sometimes they dreamed up long journeys. Their arrangements and plans for each trip would fill three or four evenings. They would imagine they were traveling around the world on a big ocean liner and that warm breezes were blowing over the water. Monkeys frisked about in palm trees. Fierce lions roared at night. Swaying easily on camelback, the globe-trotters would cross the desert. But then a cold wind blew in their faces, and they were on their way north. Seals were playing on blocks of ice. The travelers rushed across smooth ice fields, frightening away caribou. Soon they would come to the North Pole, where the wind swirled the snow round and round. But the adventurers weren't afraid of bad weather. Through blizzards and wind they always went on.

Sometimes they journeyed back into the past. They watched Ivan the Terrible storm Kazan or Peter the Great work as a carpenter in Holland's shipyards. They rejoiced when the Swedes were defeated at Poltava. And they crossed the Alps with Suvorov, becoming dizzy as they looked into the terrible precipices that yawned beneath their feet.

Their journey lasted on and on while the wind howled and whistled through the forest, while trees bent and moaned, and while snow drifted to the top of the frosty cottage windows.

Tired from playing hard all day, Lena would fall asleep. Then they dropped the burning pine splinter, which had been used to light their little room, into a bucket of water. The day would come to an end.

Wolves came near the house at night. Their tracks could be clearly seen in the morning. Solomin and Kolya had to make a strong lock for the cattle shed and board the window up so that wolves couldn't get their cow.

The first winter passed. Just before spring, the old schoolteacher went to the village and bought some planting potatoes with the money he got from selling two shirts out of the seemingly inexhaustible supply of things in their trunk. As soon as the snow melted, fieldwork began.

They worked from early morning till late in the evening without straightening their backs. Their hands were so blistered they bled. It took them a long time to fall asleep at night, their bodies ached so. In the end, they cultivated a good-sized strip of land and set out the planting potatoes. In June they mowed hay. Lena brought water to the tired mowers and took the cow to pasture herself.

When autumn came again, the harvest turned out to be a good one. They had a full cellar of potatoes. However, they couldn't figure out how to grind the rye so that it could be made into bread. They tried pounding it in a wooden mortar, but that process was very slow and difficult. Finally they decided to boil a thick kasha from the rye and eat it in place of bread. They baked real bread only on holidays.

Lena remembered less and less about her former life. She couldn't even recall her last name very well. When Grandfather told her one day that her last name was Solomina, Lena believed him and asked no questions.

The second winter was considerably easier. There were enough potatoes. In addition, they had five poods of smoked fish and dried mushrooms. Life became orderly and peaceful.

Every evening "night school" was held. Now Lena learned, too. Toward springtime she was able to read, although not very fast, to tell the truth. She could even print the letters of the alphabet.

Unfortunately, there were neither books, nor paper, nor ink at their forest home. Lena learned to read from a tattered book entitled *Forestry*, which they had found in the cupboard. The only pencil they had was almost used up. Ivan Ignatyevich's stories, although they were interesting and educational, could not take the place of primers. Moreover, the time had come to study more advanced material. These problems were often discussed. Finally they decided that as soon as it got warm Ivan Ignatyevich would go to Zapolsk to see his old friend, Doctor Krechetov. He would try to get some primers, paper, pen, and ink from him.

3

Some Surprising News

Solomin didn't manage to get to Zapolsk until autumn. In the spring, fieldwork had to be started. His trip was put off later on because of the haying and gardening. Kolya couldn't handle all this work alone. It wasn't until September, after everything had been harvested, the cellar filled with potatoes and vegetables, the rye threshed, and enough wood chopped for the winter that Solomin finally set out.

He felt uneasy as he walked toward his hometown. He hadn't been there for over two years. What had become of his friends and neighbors and his former pupils in the meantime? Which ones were no longer alive, and how would those who were still living greet him? Last, but not least, what would they tell him?

He had heard almost nothing about what was happening in the world for over two years now. News trickled into the village where he traded very slowly. And he had been afraid to ask questions, because he didn't want to attract attention to himself.

But Ivan Ignatyevich felt he could no longer remain in hiding. As a matter of fact, that conclusion was the main reason for his undertaking this risky trip. He left the road a short distance from town and stayed in the forest till dusk. When it began to get dark, he came out onto the road again. The streets of Zapolsk were empty and quiet. Everyone's windows were closed tightly, and curtains were pulled across them.

He stopped in front of Doctor Krechetov's house. It seemed empty. Solomin couldn't bring himself to knock for quite a while.

When it came right down to bare facts, what did he know about Krechetov now? Maybe the doctor wasn't living there any longer, and Hitler's officers or officials were living there instead. Then he'd really be in trouble! But to stand out in the street for any length of time was dangerous, too. He could be arrested.

Solomin decided to knock. The door didn't open for a long time. Finally he heard the cautious shuffling of feet and a woman's voice ask, "Who's there?"

"I must see Yevgeny Andreyevich," Solomin answered in a low voice.

There was whispering behind the door. A man's voice asked, "Who wants to see me?"

"Yevgeny Andreyevich," said Solomin, "it's me— Ivan Ignatyevich. Open up, please."

A bolt scraped, and the door was opened. Doctor Krechetov, who had become thin and gray, stood looking out into the darkness. He stepped forward abruptly, grabbed Solomin by the hand, and pulled him into the hallway, closing the door and cautiously bolting it. Putting his arms around Ivan Ignatyevich's shoulders, he embraced him heartily and kissed him three times.

Then he glanced at the door suspiciously and asked, "Did anybody see you? No? Well, good. Come in."

Within five minutes the two old friends were seated in easy chairs in Krechetov's study, smiling and looking at one another as if they couldn't get their fill.

"You're alive!" Krechetov marveled over and over again. "Oh, Ivan, Ivan, we two old fellows are still living."

They both were so glad to see each other and so overcome with happiness that they couldn't begin any kind of sensible conversation.

Aleksandra Andreyevna, Krechetov's sister, put a

linen tablecloth on the table and brought in some bread, a plate of salted milk mushrooms, a jar of soaked red bilberries, and the samovar. Solomin never had liked the spiteful little old woman, who was envious and gossipy, but now he was glad to see even her. Aleksandra Andreyevna poured tea into big cups decorated with blue flowers and left the room.

A lamp hung over the little table. Its light seemed amazingly bright to Solomin, who was used to lighting his forest cottage with pine splinters. The samovar whistled softly. The windows were shuttered, and the blinds were drawn tightly. For a second it seemed to Ivan Ignatyevich that the last two years had been a dream. Perhaps there was no war, no Nazi occupation, and no life in the wild forest. Maybe this moment was simply a meeting of two old friends to play a game of chess, drink tea, and have a little chat.

Suddenly Krechetov started and listened. "Do you hear?" he asked. "It must be the patrol."

The sound of footsteps could, indeed, be heard coming up the street. Hollow thuds passed the house and faded away. Then Krechetov became light-hearted again, took a sip of tea, and looked at Solomin happily.

No, the old schoolteacher thought, the war and the occupation are here. Nazis are all over town, and we are hiding in holes like wild animals.

"Well," said Yevgeny Andreyevich, "tell me about everything."

Ivan Ignatyevich nodded. "I will, later on," he said. "I've been living such an isolated life all this time that I don't know about anything. First fill me in on what's been happening in the world."

Yevgeny Andreyevich glanced sideways at the window, then leaned across the table and whispered, "They've been defeated in the vicinity of Moscow!"

"Is that so?" Solomin asked in a whisper.

Krechetov nodded and burst out laughing, rubbing his hands together. He leaned toward Solomin again. "In the Stalingrad area, Hitler's army was surrounded and. . . ." He made an expressive gesture.

"It was destroyed?" asked Ivan Ignatyevich.

Krechetov nodded and laughed. "Then again in the North Caucasus . . . and near Taganrog . . . and the Donets Basin and the Ukraine." His eyes were smiling. He was triumphant.

"What now?" asked Solomin.

"They're being driven out!" whispered Yevgeny Andreyevich.

"Where to?"

"Back to Germany."

The two old friends looked at one another and laughed.

"Some soldiers!" said Solomin. "Some 'masters of the world!'"

"True, true." Krechetov had a secretive look. "Wait a second, and I'll show you something."

He glanced at the window again and listened for footsteps in the street. Then he took a little map of Europe, which had been ripped from a geography book, out of a box. The old friends leaned over it.

"Just be careful," said Krechetov. "We mustn't make any kind of mark on it. The Nazis search our houses quite often, and they look over the maps carefully."

The two of them examined the map for a long time, whispering to one another excitedly. Looking at the winding lines that were rivers and the little dots that represented towns, Solomin imagined the movement of two enormous armies, the smoke and flames of great battles, and the nearness of freedom.

Afterward Yevgeny Andreyevich Krechetov hid the map again. "Now tell me about yourself," he said.

While sipping tea, Solomin began to tell him in a

leisurely manner that fate had abandoned a little girl at his door, that he had searched for and found Kolya, that they had moved to a cottage in the forest where they had gradually learned to eke out a living by farming, and that the three of them lived just like Robinson Crusoe on his desert island.

The amazed Krechetov listened very attentively, nodding enthusiastically and jumping up uneasily to pace the floor now and then. "I envy you," he said, when Ivan Ignatyevich had finished his story. "How happy I would be to live like you and not have to hear these patrols walking by my windows all the time!"

Growing pensive, he sat down, then sighed and put down his empty cup with a sharp movement. "Well," he concluded, "enough of that! The more you think about it, the more upset you get. What do you plan to do with Lena? Her father might still be alive."

"If he's alive," Solomin answered, "we'll find him after the war. It would be hopeless to look for him now."

"Yes, of course," Yevgeny Andreyevich answered thoughtfully. "You say he's a colonel and his unit was stationed here? What is his last name? I may have heard it by chance."

"Rogachov," Solomin replied.

"Rogachov?" Krechetov asked again. "And his first and middle name?"

"Stepan Grigoryevich."

"Stepan Grigoryevich?" Krechetov moved forward. "And you mean to say you haven't heard anything about him?"

"No, nothing."

"Well, I must say, you really do live like a bear in its den!"

"What do you mean? What has happened to him?"

"Nothing, except that Stepan Grigoryevich Rogachov is now one of the most famous generals in the Red Army."

There was a pause. The two men looked at one another.

"Listen," said Solomin, "this is very dangerous. What if the Germans find out that Rogachov's daughter is living with me?"

"Naturally it's dangerous," Krechetov agreed. "There's even a rumor going around that Rogachov's family was here in Zapolsk. It's a good thing nobody knows what became of you. They all think you were killed in the bombing."

"I would like to see some of my old friends. . . ." Solomin said hesitantly.

"No, no." Krechetov waved his hands. "Not a chance of it! Don't forget that everyone is watched. The Germans listen to every word. I'm going to ask you not to tell even my sister anything about this. Of course, she wouldn't inform on you, but you know women. They're apt to let something slip out accidentally. That reminds me. I'd better have her heat up the samovar again."

He flung open the door, and they heard a groan. Aleksandra Andreyevna Krechetova stood in the doorway, holding her hand against her forehead. "You've given me a nice bump, I must say!" she complained.

"Aleksandra, what were you doing behind the door?" Krechetov asked in surprise.

"I wanted to reheat the samovar. It's probably cold by now." She grabbed the samovar and left the room indignantly.

The old friends talked till dawn. Krechetov told Solomin everything he knew about Rogachov, who had become well-known in a battle near Moscow. General Rogachov's units struck one of the major blows of the war outside of Stalingrad, and from that time on the name Rogachov thundered on many fronts and in many battles. He passed like a whirlwind through the Donets Basin. Later on the liberated sections of the Ukraine greeted the man called General Rogachov with wild enthusiasm.

Muffling his voice, Krechetov sang a song about Rogachov. This song was popular in freed territory, and it was known even in occupied Zapolsk. Krechetov sang very quietly, almost in a whisper. He had to be careful. Not long ago the Nazis had shot a girl for singing the song.

"He is here on our front," said Yevgeny Andreyevich. "His troops will take Zapolsk."

All the next day, while Solomin was visiting, Krechetov forbade him even to go over to the windows.

When it began to get dark, Ivan Ignatyevich left town. He carried with him a complete set of primers and a supply of paper, pens, pencils, and ink. Krechetov had asked people he knew for all these things on various pretexts. As Solomin walked along, it seemed to him that everybody he met looked at him suspiciously. Before he went into the forest, he took a long look around and turned only when he was convinced there was no one else on the road.

He didn't say anything to the children about Rogachov. Life at their forest home went on as usual. Winter came and snow covered the cottage almost up to the roof. They could spare more time this year for studies. Kolya learned decimals and fractions, and he read from real history and geography books. On Sundays they had exams.

The children had become quite used to living in the forest. Kolya wasn't afraid of mysterious forest beasts anymore. Now it was Ivan Ignatyevich who slept poorly. He was bothered by rheumatism all winter long. His legs swelled up, and he had a hard time walking to the lake. As he tossed from side to side without sleeping, the old man thought, If we can only hold out until our own troops come! I'll give Lena back to her father, and Kolya will go to school. Then I can rest.

He would doze off thinking these thoughts, which he couldn't shake off either in his dreams or in his waking hours. It seemed to him that the Nazis were coming to their little home to surround it and take Lena away. He developed the habit of looking intently into the forest several times a day, imagining that something had appeared among the trees for a moment. He would squint his nearsighted eyes and ask Kolya if he saw anybody, distrustfully shaking his head when Kolya said no one was there. Then he would stare again until his eyes began to hurt.

But that winter passed safely and happily. Spring came, then summer. Finally it was the end of June, 1944.

4

A Stranger

The sun was sinking behind the forest after a hot day in July. It was getting cool, and fog was settling in the lowlands. A fish jumped and splashed about in the little lake as evening drew near.

A short, stocky man, wearing boots and linen trousers with a peasant-style shirt, came walking up the forest path. Despite the fact that he was dressed like a peasant, something in his face and gait seemed city bred, and his coarse linen clothes looked unnatural on him.

He had only one arm. His empty left sleeve was tucked into his belt. A knapsack hung from his right shoulder. The man pressed it to his side with his elbow so that it wouldn't hang loose.

The lake flashed through the trees like a mirror. After making a turn, the little path went along the slope of the hill. Aspens and fir trees gave way to birches. Then the gray wall of the shed could be seen from behind white birch trunks. A potato field stretched out on one side, and stalks of rye, looking like silver in the gray dusk, grew on the other side.

Two enormous, solitary birch trees towered over the summit of the hill. The cottage, built of thick logs with its roof and shingles darkened with age, stood between them. The crimson sun, drifting across the sky, was reflected in the little windows of the cottage.

The stranger took off his cap, then wiped the sweat from his forehead with his one arm as he calmly glanced around.

Ivan Ignatyevich sat on the porch without moving, looking at his visitor suspiciously. Solomin's gray hair, which hadn't been cut for a long time, hung down almost to his shoulders. His beard, ending in a long, sharp point, dangled down on his chest. He seemed like a character from a fairy tale, and everything around him was storybooklike: the lonely cottage on top of the hill, the silver lake below, and the mysteriously silent forest.

"Good evening, granddad!" the visitor called in a loud, merry voice.

"Good evening," the old man answered unwillingly.

"Does Ivan Ignatyevich Solomin live here?"

"Yes."

The stranger looked very closely at the old man. "Are you he?"

"No."

"I see." He sat down on the porch beside the old man. "Who are you, granddad? Do you live here with Solomin?"

"No."

"Then where do you live?"

The old man pointed somewhere into the depths of the forest.

"In the village?"

Solomin shook his head.

"Just in the forest?" the stranger kept questioning.

The old man nodded.

"Then you're a kind of hermit?"

The old man nodded again.

"Where is Solomin?"

"He went to the lake to fish . . . for a week or two." The old schoolteacher spoke the words as if he were choosing them with difficulty.

"Why are you here?"

"He asked me to keep a watch on the place."

"I understand. And is this lake far away?"

The old man shrugged his shoulders.

"Don't you know? Did he take a little girl with him?"

The stranger overplayed his part. He asked about the little girl too indifferently. And although he turned his face away quickly, he didn't succeed in hiding the intent look that he had given the old man. Solomin didn't indicate he had noticed that look.

"Who?" he asked. There was no expression on his face. He looked the same as he had before the man asked the question.

"A little girl," said the visitor, "who lives with him. She may be adopted."

"Oh, yes," the old man said, drawing his words out slowly. "A little girl does live with him. Probably his granddaughter."

"Well, did he take her with him?"

"Of course."

"So. . . . And is the lake far from here?"

The old man shrugged his shoulders again.

"Oh, yes, I forgot that you don't know. Does that mean he'll be back in two weeks? I see. . . ."

The stranger took a pouch of tobacco and some cigarette paper out of his pocket. "Do you smoke?" he asked, holding the pouch out to the old man.

Solomin's face brightened. Something similar to a smile crossed it, and he extended his hand for the **tobacco.**

"We both like to smoke, I guess," said the visitor. "It's boring to be without a cigarette, isn't it? It's a nice relaxation, but tobacco is hard to come by and very expensive nowadays."

He pretended not to notice the old man's hands stretched toward the tobacco. "I must see Solomin," he said absentmindedly. "You see, I'm an old pupil of his. He taught me in school. He knows me quite well. I simply must give him a bit of information. It is very important for him to know. Can't you remember where the lake is, granddad? I will give you my tobacco. There are three glassfuls in this pouch. What do you say?"

The old man's face clearly reflected indecision. Apparently he didn't want to say where Solomin was fishing, but the tobacco was temptingly near, and a whole three glassfuls at that.

He sighed as though regretting his weakness and said, "Follow this path to the lake below. Then go to the right. Walk on for five versts, and you'll come to a country road. Take a left on that road. It's three versts to a river from there. On the riverbank, you'll find a path that leads to a big lake. Go on for ten versts, and you'll find a hut on the shore of the lake. A woodcutter built it. They are staying there."

The visitor cheered up. Skillfully manipulating

his only hand, he untied his knapsack and took out a bundle of tobacco.

"Here. Take it," he said, "and smoke to your heart's content. So it will be twenty versts in all?"

The old man didn't seem to hear him. He quickly rolled a cigarette and went into the cottage to light it. The stranger tied up his knapsack, tossed it over his shoulder, and walked hurriedly down the path. He was soon hidden by the trees. Twigs snapped under his feet. Then the snapping stopped. His small figure appeared now and then beside the lake below and finally disappeared in the thick foliage and brush.

The door of the cottage slowly opened, and Solomin came out onto the porch. He stood there for a moment, looking intently into the forest. Then he gave three loud calls, which sounded like the song of an oriole. The forest was silent. Suddenly another oriole answered with three short cries. The old man waited and watched, squinting because he couldn't see very well in the twilight. Once again twigs snapped on the path. A little boy and girl stepped from behind the trees. The boy seemed to be about twelve years old. He walked with an even, confident gait, as people do who are accustomed to the forest. His face was weather-beaten and tanned, so his eyes seemed especially light—almost white.

The little girl was seven. She had a turned-up nose with three freckles on the end. Her eyes were so big that they seemed wide open in surprise. Two pigtails bounced on her shoulders.

"Are we late?" asked the boy.

"We saw a sheatfish in the lake!" the girl interrupted.

"Yes," said the boy, "and was it ever big!"

"Fierce, with long whiskers!" the girl broke in again.

"Yes. We heard a woodpecker."

"When we went near, it flew away."

"I found a new raspberry patch."

"Its enormous!" the girl added.

"And Lena ate so many raspberries," said the boy, "I don't understand why she isn't sick."

"Really?" asked the old man. "Now she won't want to eat anything else sweet. I have some honey, and I was going to ask her to make us some pancakes."

"That's all right," Lena was quick to say. "I can eat a little honey, too. Is the oven heated?"

"It's hot, and there's a pile of wood beside it.

While you are cooking, Kolya and I will sit here and chat."

Lena went into the cottage.

"We don't have much time, Kolya," said the old man after a moment of silence, "and I have a lot to tell you. I didn't think we would have to part so soon. . . ."

5

A Long Journey

Shadows thickened over the forest. Pale stars peeked through the still-bright sky as the grandfather and grandson talked on.

"I always thought Lena was my cousin," said Kolya. "Why did you deceive me, Grandfather?"

"You were still young. Besides, what would it have changed? We have no time to talk about it now. Think how important it is to the Nazis to capture Rogachov's daughter. Their revenge would be terrible. How could I look Rogachov in the face if he came here and asked why I didn't protect her?"

"That couldn't happen, Grandfather," said Kolya. "What do you mean? We will be sure to protect her. Who would find out she is here? There aren't any people around, and I know places where no one could find us."

He glanced around. The forest surrounded them.

The moon had come out and was shining through the bent, white branches of four birch trees, which were casting eerie shadows. In the ghostly light, the branches seemed to be hands, and the tree trunks looked like the bodies of strange forest monsters.

"There are no Germans here in the forest," the boy said uncertainly. "No one will find out she's here."

The old man, lowering his voice, answered, "They have already found out, Kolya. I don't know how. But they know she's here."

"What makes you think that?"

"A man visited me today. He was dressed like a peasant, but he wasn't one. He had a city accent, and his knapsack wasn't tied as the peasants tie theirs. He thought I was supposed to watch over the cottage. He was a strange man, short with a good-natured—too good-natured—face and no left arm."

"Why did he come?" Kolya whispered.

"He asked about the girl living with Solomin," the old man whispered back.

"What did you tell him?"

"I told him Solomin had taken the children fishing. I sent him twenty versts away to look for us.

Twenty versts there and twenty versts back. He'll return by tomorrow evening."

"What will we do?"

"Tomorrow evening you and Lena will be far away from here."

"What about you?"

The old man was silent. He looked tired. "I will stay," he said. "You know I can't walk very well. I would only be a hindrance to you. You're a big boy now, Kolya. I think you know just as much as a city boy. Besides, you've spent three years in the forest. You aren't a coward, and you're quick to catch on. Are you afraid?"

"No, I'm not afraid. Where will we go?"

The old man shrugged. "What can I tell you? It would be best to take Lena across the front line and give her to her father, General Stepan Grigorye-vich Rogachov, or perhaps to some other command-ing officer or soldier. If you can't do that (and it would be very difficult to do, Kolya), then you must take her to the partisans. They are people who are on our side and who work secretly in areas occupied by Nazis. Where they are, I don't know. They hide in the forests. You must find them."

"I understand."

"If you don't succeed in doing so, hide among the people and wait until our own soldiers come."

"All right. Where do you think we should go now?"

"Go to Zapolsk, to Doctor Krechetov. I won't write to him because it's dangerous. If he doesn't recognize you—after all, you've grown these last few years—tell him that you're my grandson. But tell him in private when there are no strangers around."

"I understand."

"Don't tell Lena who her father is. She is little and could give our secret away."

"All right, Grandfather."

"I didn't think," the old man repeated, "we would have to part so soon. . . ."

"Supper!" Lena called to them. She stood in the doorway, thin and tiny, with her two braids hanging down her back. "The pancakes are ready! Get the honey to pour on them, Grandfather."

After supper they told Lena she would set out on a journey with Kolya the next day. At first she was worried, but her grandfather and cousin had such happy faces that the forthcoming trip began to seem very interesting. They gathered their things together merrily and tied them into two little bundles. They went to bed in high spirits and awoke the next morning feeling the same way.

But parting with Grandfather was sad. Lena broke into tears while kissing him good-by. The old man confidently told her they would see one another again before long. The little girl dried her eyes and cheered up once more.

It was a beautiful day. The dew was sparkling. When the birds awoke, they wished one another such a joyful good morning that the journey seemed still more inviting than it had the day before.

They took leave of Grandfather by the lake. The old man stood for a long time, following them with his eyes. They walked along hand in hand, the tall boy and the little girl, each carrying a stick over the shoulder with a bundle tied on the end. They were soon hidden by the trees, but their lively voices could still be heard for a long while afterward. Then the sound of their voices faded.

Solomin sat on the little porch all day. He sighed, moved his lips, then sighed again. In the evening the one-armed man approached the cottage once more. Solomin looked at him indifferently.

The stranger said, "You played a clever trick on me, Ivan Ignatyevich Solomin, but you will come to regret it deeply."

6

The Chase

Lena and Kolya walked down the forest path. Soon the lake was behind them. The path came out onto a country road, which skirted a dead pine grove. Up to this point the land was familiar to them. They used to run and play here. Why, once Kolya had hidden behind that big pine tree and frightened Lena half to death. Farther on, however, unknown territory began, a land in which they had never been. It was a little frightening but very interesting. They kept making wonderful discoveries. For example, Lena found an enormous anthill. There had been none so large near their cottage. Turning off the road, they came upon a spot where red and white mushrooms were growing. The children quickly picked so many that they had no place to put them all.

Toward evening they came to the village. Kolya decided to go around it to avoid unpleasant meetings.

This area was a land of forests, hills, and lakes. The children spent the next day swimming in a wonderful lake. Later on they built a campfire, cleaned their mushrooms, and boiled them in a kettle. Kolya cut a branch to make a fishing rod (he had a hook and line with him) and caught about ten silvery-green fish, which made a tasty soup. After dinner the children fell asleep and napped for two hours.

The sun had already dipped toward the west when Kolya awoke. Lena probably would have slept longer if he hadn't awakened her. They took another short swim in the lake, then went on.

At sunset they came to a highway. Kolya started to teach Lena how to answer questions people would ask her. It wasn't so simple to think up a story about themselves. They decided to say they lived in Alekseyevka, since there was a village by that name fifty kilometers away, and that their parents had been taken to Germany; consequently, they were making their way to Doctor Krechetov, a relative in Zapolsk.

They met people along the way from time to time. For the most part, they were peasants. Once, however, a Nazi officer and a woman rode by in a car. He was explaining something and pointing at the forest. The woman looked frightened and miserable.

A log and mud dugout, enclosed with barbed wire, stood at a bend in the road. There German soldiers were sitting around smoking. They kept glancing indifferently at the road. They felt safe in daytime.

An old man was driving a sow and her three piglets past the dugout. One of the soldiers got up and with a quick, experienced movement grabbed one of the piglets. The little pig squealed despairingly and jerked its legs as the soldier tossed it into the dugout with a sweep of his arm. The old man gave him a frightened look, but the soldier didn't even glance at him. Whipping his pigs with a long switch, the old man hurried on.

Dusk came. The children left the highway and went into the forest. They chose a spot that was a little drier and a little more level than the others, raked up a pile of leaves, buried themselves in it, and went to sleep. Night came quietly. Sometimes a vehicle passed by on the highway. Once shooting erupted some distance away, but it stopped just as suddenly as it had begun. In the morning they ate a bit of bread and walked on.

Kolya decided to take the steamboat to town.

He knew from what his grandfather had said that the highway led to a pier, where the steamboat going to Zapolsk pulled in every evening.

As they continued walking down the road, things became livelier. There were more and more villages. Traffic got heavier, and German patrols marched back and forth.

That day they bought some milk from an old lady. At first when they asked whether or not she had some milk for sale, the old woman screamed at them.

"Where would I get milk?" she asked indignantly. "My own family has nothing to eat. My grandchildren haven't seen a drop of milk in weeks."

Then she softened and asked who they were and where they came from. They told about their parents, whom the Nazis had taken to Germany, and about their relative in Zapolsk. The old woman, grumbling angrily, went into her cottage and brought out an earthenware pot of milk. She didn't want to take any money for it. Suddenly she began to scold again. The children were afraid of her and quickly went away. They puzzled over whether she was a good or bad person for quite a while, but they couldn't decide one way or the other.

Lena was tired yet held up like a trooper. When

Kolya offered to stop for a rest, she refused, but he decided it was time all the same. They lay down in some bushes, slept for an hour or so, and went on. The highway went down a steep hill. At the bottom they saw a wide river gliding smoothly between wooded banks, a big village, and a pier. But most important, they saw the steamboat approaching, putting on speed. Fortunately for them, getting down the hill was easy.

Suddenly they heard the rumble of wheels behind them and the loud cry, "Get out of the way!" A cart, pulled by a big bay horse, was rushing down the road. A gray-haired man was holding the reins and clucking to the horse. On the hay in back, bobbing up and down and being jolted to and fro, was a man dressed in boots and a shirt with a rope belt. He looked intently at the children and was just about to raise his hand to stop the horse when he thought better of it. The cart rushed by and was soon hidden behind some houses.

Kolya and Lena weren't too late after all. The ticket teller sold them third-class tickets, and they quickly ran down the gangplank. The cart that had passed them was beside the pier, and the man who had driven the horse was now holding a sack of oats up to its nose.

7

An Unexpected Neighbor

The lower deck was jammed with people. They were sitting on suitcases, sacks, and right on the deck itself. With difficulty Kolya and Lena found a place, finally having to ask a woman to push over and make room for them. The steamboat whistled, gave a blast, and started up. Water began to churn beneath its wheels, and it lurched first forward, then backward. Once they had drifted past the dock, they steamed by houses, trees, and steep riverbanks.

Lena was seeing a steamboat for the first time in her life. She jumped at every blast, fearfully grabbing Kolya's hand when they steamed by the pier. She watched the moving wheels and connecting rods in the engine room as if she were bewitched. Every now and then she tugged at Kolya and whispered in his ear.

"What's that round thing?"

"A life preserver," Kolya whispered back.

"And what's that thick, tall thing?"

"The smokestack."

The woman sitting next to them kept staring. Finally she spoke. "Why do you keep whispering, children?" she began. "You should be running around deck and going up to the captain to see how he runs things. Nowadays only Germans are allowed there, of course. But there used to be Russians around. There were Russians on the top deck, Russians on the lower deck—Russians everywhere. The Germans stayed in Germany."

People sitting near the woman began to look. Some even made a sign to her. They seemed to be saying, "It would be better to be quiet, silly, than to get yourself into trouble." But the woman was unable to hold her tongue.

"I know," she said loudly in answer to the warning glances. "I know that I shouldn't speak out, but I can't help it. My husband always warned me to be quiet, until they arrested him. And I would be happy to, but it doesn't work out that way. The only thing that saves me is that these devils don't understand a word of Russian, and I haven't come across a Russian who has turned traitor yet. But if I do, it'll be the end of me." She smiled sadly and stopped talking.

All this time a German soldier was walking around

deck, morosely glancing first to the right, then to the left. No one looked at him. No one seemed even to notice him, but the conversation on deck suddenly died down. There was nothing for him to find fault with, so the soldier walked by.

"What ill wind blew him here?" the woman asked angrily after he had passed.

It got dark and quite a few people began to settle down to sleep. Some put sacks under their heads, others laid their heads on neighbors' shoulders, and still others tried to stretch out their legs somehow. Kolya and Lena watched lighted cottage windows, trees bending over the water, and the riverbanks drifting by. How wide the world seemed and how small the little piece of earth they had lived on for three years! There were settlements, villages, and towns scattered all over the world with people living in every house. Each person had his own life story, perhaps even more extraordinary than Kolya's and Lena's.

Water gurgled monotonously beneath the wheels as the engine puffed and steamed along. Several people were already asleep. Each one was probably dreaming his own dream—happy in some cases, and sad in others.

Someone (it was too dark to see whom) was

playing softly on the balalaika. The invisible musician began one tune, then stopped without finishing it. He went on to another and stopped again as if he were thinking and passing from one thought to another. Then he began to sing softly. Kolya didn't know the song and had never heard it before. Suddenly he shuddered, for he distinctly heard the name of Rogachov among the words.

"What's the matter with you?" Lena asked lazily. She had just fallen into a light slumber a few moments before.

"Nothing," Kolya answered. "Go to sleep."

He began to listen with strained attention. The singer's voice was hushed and low, but since it was quiet all around, every word of the song could be heard clearly.

The song told about the forests harboring a great grief and stalks of grain pressing against the earth out of anguish and suffering rather than because of the weight of their fruit. It told about young girls crying and old women shriveling up from unhappiness while their boys and men, far away from their native land amidst fire and death, are remembering their homes and longing for their own villages. Then, through forests and swamps, through walls of fire and metal, Rogachov's regiments come to the rescue. Days turn to nights, and nights turn to days as the regiments of General Rogachov come closer and closer to their homeland.

In the semidarkness, the singer softly repeated the refrain, "General Rogachov leads his regiments nearer and nearer to their homeland."

Then he suddenly ran his fingers over the strings and sang some merry folk songs.

Once again the German soldier passed along the lower deck, walking over feet and bodies as though they were slabs of wood.

"Who is this Rogachov he is singing about?" Lena asked quietly. Apparently she hadn't been asleep and had heard the song.

"Go to sleep," Kolya answered. "He is a famous Soviet general."

"Who will soon come here with his regiments," said a voice above Kolya's ear.

Kolya turned. The man who had passed them in the cart sat down beside them.

"By the way, they say Rogachov isn't very far away at this very moment," he added.

People all around them were sleeping in odd and uncomfortable positions. They were snoring and mumbling in their sleep. Evidently no one had overheard.

"He's right near here?" asked Kolya.

"That's what they say," the stranger answered. "But who knows whether or not it's true?"

Kolya was very flattered that a grown-up was chatting with him so seriously about matters of war. The stranger immediately passed on to another subject.

"Are you going far?" he asked.

"To Zapolsk," said Kolya.

"On business or what?"

Kolya told him the story he and Lena had made up on the way. The stranger was very sympathetic and said that their relatives in town would certainly help them. As a precaution, Kolya didn't give Doctor Krechetov's name.

The man opened his knapsack, took out a little package, and said while turning it around, "Let me treat you to some sugar."

There was something odd about his movements. Despite the fact that it was dark and difficult to distinguish his figure, Kolya kept feeling there was some kind of abnormality or irregularity in the stranger's actions.

"Go ahead and take some," he said.

Why does he do everything with one hand? Kolya thought. His heart sank.

Someone nearby lit a match and began to smoke. In the short flash of wavering light, Kolya immediately caught a glimpse of an empty sleeve tucked into a belt, linen trousers, a knapsack, and a good-natured—too good-natured—face.

Lena accepted the sugar, but Kolya's mouth went dry and his heart sank even lower. The match went out. It was dark again. While the stranger was persuading Lena to take another piece, the distraught Kolya thought frantically about what he could do. Just then the steamboat gave a blast. Lena shuddered, then laughed and shouted something. It was impossible to make out her words, because the noise drowned them out. Dim lights appeared on the riverbank.

"The pier," said the one-armed man.

"If you want, Lena, we'll go have a look around," said Kolya.

The one-armed man got up. He was going with them.

"Would you be so kind as to look after our things while we're gone?" asked Kolya.

It would be a shame to lose their things. They had packed bread and fish. But if they took their bundles, the one-armed man would go with them.

Fortunately, Kolya had some money in his pocket.

The children began to make their way across the crowded deck. The gangplank had already been let down. Lena was surprised when Kolya led her down to the pier.

"Won't the boat leave without us?" she asked.

"Never mind," Kolya answered. "Let's go!"

They walked quickly down the pier past sacks and barrels. The boat gave a blast. It didn't stop very long.

Lena was upset. "Kolya, the boat is leaving right now!"

Kolya silently dragged her along behind him. They passed little houses beside the pier and went up a steep bank. There the forest began. Ducking behind a thick birch, Kolya stopped.

"Lena," he said, "we must leave this place. That man who was sitting beside us—you saw him. He is the one-armed man. The same one we had to leave home because of."

The children silently watched as the gangplank was taken up and water started churning under the steamboat's wheels. The boat moved away from the pier, at first slowly, then faster and faster. Only when the lights of the boat disappeared around a bend in the river did the children breathe freely.

8

Zapolsk

The children would have been in Zapolsk by morning if they had stayed on the steamboat. But on foot the journey took them almost two whole days and a night. They spent the night in the forest. Although Lena was tired and begged to stay in a little village, Kolya decided to avoid populated areas.

They approached Zapolsk toward evening of the second day with their clothing torn and covered with dust. Kolya sang songs and told funny stories. Lena laughed, but Kolya felt she was laughing only to make him happy and that actually she would have liked better than anything else to go to bed and snuggle into the blankets.

The road went uphill, where gigantic pines spread their branches. The sun sank in the west, and shadows crossed the road. When the heat became less intense, the children's spirits rose.

"Kolya, how many people are there in a city? A million?" asked Lena.

"There are less than that in Zapolsk. But some cities have even more than a million."

"A billion?"

"No, there aren't that many people in any city. Four or five million maybe."

"Five million!" Lena shook her head. "And how many people live in a village? A thousand?"

"There are less than a thousand in some villages and more in others."

"A thousand people! It scares you to think about it."

The top of the hill abruptly came into view. Then the road sloped down steeply. Kolya and Lena stopped. A silver river crossed the wooded plain. Zapolsk was spread out on the bank of this river. Roofs were visible among the green treetops. Little houses of many different colors stood in rows along the bank.

It had been three years since Kolya had last seen Zapolsk. As he looked at the town, many things came to mind. There were the rafts he used to swim around. There was his three-story school building, towering high over the one-story houses. He felt sad that he had to steal into his own hometown, fearing everyone he met along the way.

"What tall buildings!" exclaimed the delighted Lena. "How many stories does that one have?"

"Three."

"It must be scary living on the top floor!"

Kolya took her by the hand. "Let's go!"

"You aren't even a little bit afraid?" Lena asked in an undertone.

"Not a bit," the boy answered with hesitation. Actually he was very uneasy.

"I'm afraid. Just a little bit, of course."

"Let's go anyway."

He walked ahead and Lena followed.

Within half an hour, they entered Zapolsk. The town was quiet and empty. Old men were no longer sitting on their little porches, and women weren't gossiping over fences. An occasional pedestrian hurried by, looking straight ahead without even glancing to the side. No one paid any attention to Kolya and Lena. Dirty and covered with dust, they looked like beggars in their rumpled clothing. At that time it was common to see beggar children roaming the streets, so they seemed no different from the others.

Any other time they would have walked along

without hurrying, looking everything over and talking about it. But they were so tired and wanted so much to rest as soon as possible that they were silent. Like the others, they didn't even cast a sideways glance. Besides they were afraid. If there was danger on the forest road, they could always leave the road and hide behind some trees or in some bushes. But there was nowhere to hide in town. They were surrounded by houses where strangers lived.

Doctor Krechetov lived in a cozy one-story house with a little fence around it and a cleanly swept porch. Kolya knocked resolutely. No one answered for a long time. Then they heard footsteps. An old gray-haired woman with a thin, wrinkled face opened the door. Holding Lena firmly by the hand, Kolya stepped forward.

"We must see Doctor Krechetov," he said.

"He's not home," the old lady answered.

"When will he be home?"

The woman was silent, then suddenly said sharply, "He won't be home at all!" and closed the door.

The children looked at one another. Kolya didn't know what to do. He was so angry that he was ready to walk away without accomplishing what he wanted. Because Lena was miserable and tired, however, he decided to knock again. The door opened immediately. Apparently the old woman had been standing behind it.

"What do you want?" she asked sourly.

"Listen," said Kolya, "it is very important that we see the doctor. Please tell us where we can find him."

"Why do you pester me?" the woman shouted. "I told you he isn't here and won't be here. Do you understand? He won't be here! Now go away!"

She slammed the door so hard that the children involuntarily winced. Kolya almost burst into tears. He was very tired. He would have given anything to be home just then. Lena would be asleep with the palm of her hand placed under her cheek, and he would dive under the quilts, which were tucked tightly around his bed, and stretch out to sleep.

Lena tugged at his hand. "Well, never mind," she said. "Let's go."

They walked down the deserted street without looking at one another. A dog yelped lazily at them from behind a gate. Some boys were rushing down a side street, throwing a football back and forth.

"Jump!" one of them shouted.

"Got it!" another answered.

Kolya and Lena didn't see or hear anything.

"Children! Children!" someone behind them shouted.

At first Kolya didn't even think the call could have anything to do with them. But the voice repeated persistently, "Children! Children! Wait a minute!"

They turned. The old lady who had just chased them away was running after them, panting breathlessly. She stopped, catching her breath with difficulty.

"Oof!" she exclaimed. "My heart is so bad I can't even run anymore." Then she asked in a surly voice, "Why do you want Doctor Krechetov?"

Kolya was silent. The need to confide in this unfriendly, evil old woman was dreadful. But it would be even more terrible to go on to heaven knows where and lose their only hope of meeting friends in a town in which there were so many enemies.

"Well?" the old lady asked again. "Speak up, or I'll go away."

"I am the grandson of Ivan Ignatyevich Solomin," Kolya said quietly. "And this is his granddaughter, Lena."

The old woman started and cast a frightened

look all around. "Be quiet!" she said. "Is it necessary to scream so? I decided it was you right away. Don't you recognize me? I am Aleksandra Andreyevna Krechetova, the sister of Yevgeny Andreyevich Krechetov."

"No, I didn't recognize you. I was still young when I used to know you. Where is Yevgeny Andreyevich?"

"Sh-h-h!" The old woman shook her finger threateningly. "They'll hear you all the way down the other end of the street." She put her lips close to Kolya's ear and whispered in hurried agitation without completing her sentences, "They hung him. Understand? Arrested, then hung. He used to listen to Moscow on the radio . . . read leaflets. . . . Understand? Only you mustn't say anything about it."

She shook her finger again. Her gray hair was all disheveled, and her eyes glared. "You must be quiet," she said breathlessly. "Do you understand? Quiet!" Saliva drooled down the sides of her mouth.

She's crazy! thought Kolya, stepping back.

The old woman drew him to her. "Why did you leave your home in the forest?" she asked. "Are they chasing you?"

"No." Kolya decided he must hide the truth from her. "Why would they chase us? We haven't done anything."

But clearly Aleksandra Andreyevna already knew everything. "Didn't they tell the girl?" she asked.

Kolya pretended he didn't understand. "Tell her what?"

Krechetova stamped her foot angrily. "Don't play the fool, boy! Did they tell her about her father?"

Lena looked at the woman with wide-open, frightened eyes. Kolya was scared, too. Lena mustn't find out who her father was.

"Sh-h-h-!" he said. "They didn't tell her anything."

The old lady nodded. "Yes, of course. . . ." Looking at Lena, she became lost in thought. Her stare made Lena uncomfortable. It was such a cold, slightly mocking look.

"Aleksandra Andreyevna," said Kolya. "How could the Germans know about Lena? After all Grandfather told only your brother."

"I don't know," the old woman said. "How would I know? Why do you ask me?"

She avoided Kolya's eyes. But he looked steadily at her. It seemed to him that he could guess how the Nazis found out. "How do you know about

Lena's father?" he asked. "You weren't taking part in the conversation."

Without answering his question, the old lady began to mumble, "Three officers live in our apartment. I wash their clothes, prepare their meals, and tidy up the rooms. And I tremble, boy. Day and night I tremble! I'm an old woman. They can do what they want with me. I try not to make them angry. I walk quietly, smile, prepare what they like. . . . What can I do? I'm an old woman."

Kolya was getting nervous. Run! he thought. Run fast! But how? The old woman will scream and call the Nazis.

He stood there, not knowing what to do, while Aleksandra Andreyevna Krechetova kept shaking her head, smiling her strange smile and repeating, "Day and night I tremble. Day and night. . . ."

9

To the Rescue

Just then someone called Krechetov's sister. "Hey, old lady!" a man's sharp voice distinctly demanded.

Aleksandra Andreyevna started and turned.

It is hard to believe anyone's face could change so much in a single second. The old woman's confusion disappeared, and a sugary smile appeared in its place. She straightened her tousled hair and, bowing and nodding, hurried toward the house.

"I'm coming. Coming," she mumbled. She looked as though she were bowing down to the earth in humble admission of her guilt. "That's right. Scold me. What a stupid old woman I am to waste my time chatting!"

A man wearing a German officer's uniform leaned out the window of Doctor Krechetov's house. He immediately looked past Krechetova straight at Kolya and Lena. He raised to his eyes a pair of binoculars, which were hanging around his neck, and looked more closely at the children.

When he took the binoculars away, he yelled shrilly, "Hey, *Kinder!* Children!"

There was no time to think. "Let's run!" said Kolya. Pulling Lena by the hand, he quickly dragged her after him.

They turned a corner and found themselves on a shady side street. Grass was growing between the stones in the pavement. Tall trees with thick tops stood in rows along the sidewalks, and the branches of trees growing in yards and gardens stretched out over the street, too. No pedestrians were in sight. There were only four boys playing ball.

"Jump!" shouted one boy, who was throwing the ball.

"Got it!" another answered.

The boys stood stock-still when they noticed Kolya and Lena, who were being pursued with shouts and whistles.

The old lady gave us away! thought Kolya. He was seized with despair. Would they be able to escape? Would they be able to find a hiding place? Everything had gone wrong so suddenly! What would happen to Lena?

The ballplayers continued to watch the children.

Kolya ran up to them. "Fellows," he said, "they're after us!"

The boy holding the ball threw it to another. "Come with me," he said, quickly running through a gateway.

Kolya and Lena followed him into a quiet little yard. There were two lilac bushes growing over by a fence and two young birches by the porch of a little frame house. An old man was sitting on the porch tinkering away at a worn boot with an awl. He raised his head, but the running boy gave him a look, and the old man fixed his eyes on his boot again as if he hadn't noticed a thing. In a corner by a brick wall protecting the yard was a woodshed, locked with a padlock. The boy took a key out of his pocket and thrust it into the keyhole. Whistles, shouts, and running footsteps came nearer and nearer. The other boys kept playing ball on the street, just as though nothing had happened.

"Jump!" one of them shouted, throwing the ball.

"Got it!" another answered.

The shed door opened. Kolya and Lena hurriedly slipped inside. Wood, sawhorses, and a pile of brushwood, which was heaped in a corner by the brick wall, had been placed there in tidy order. Their rescuer quickly spread apart the brushwood, revealing a narrow hole that had been dug under the brick wall. The boy dived into it. His head and half his body were soon hidden on the other side of the wall. His feet were moving, and an energetic panting could be heard. Evidently he was removing some kind of obstacle which prevented his crawling through. His feet shuffled like the tail of a wiggling snake, and he disappeared into the hole.

"Climb in!" a hollow voice rang out from under the wall.

"Go ahead!" Kolya commanded.

Lena looked frightened but said nothing and unquestioningly crawled under the wall. Kolya dived in after her. They found themselves in another shed—a little bigger and better lighted. In it were more sawhorses and piles of wood. A heap of brushwood, which had been stacked against the wall, was now spread all around, revealing the other end of the hole they had just passed through.

Kolya looked to see what the boy was like who had led them on such a secret, complicated route. He was short and stocky with a wide face covered with freckles. Going over to the door, he knocked lightly on it three times. The outside padlock tinkled softly three times. The boy stood with his head tilted—listening. Light footsteps approached. The padlock clicked, and the door opened. A thin, barefoot girl in a plain cotton dress with blond bangs and a kind face stood in the doorway. She looked about ten years old.

"Niusha," said the boy, "is it quiet on your street?"

The girl nodded, stared at Kolya and Lena with curiosity, and lisped in answer, "Right now it ith, Lyotha."

"We must get them away. Let them stay in Vovka's cellar till evening. Then I'll come after them."

Niusha nodded again. Without wasting words, Lyosha dived into the hole again and, jerking his bare feet, disappeared.

The blond girl blocked the opening with brushwood and said, "Lithen, jutht don't fall behind." Then she went out into the yard.

Kolya and Lena followed. They went through a little yard, cut across a narrow street, and, after going through yet another yard, came to someone's kitchen garden on the outskirts of town. They saw fewer houses. The people who lived in them had planted potatoes, onions, cabbage, and cucumbers in orderly garden plots behind their houses, outhouses, and rubbish pits.

Niusha went ahead so confidently and quickly that Lena and Kolya could hardly keep up with her. She climbed over fences, cut corners, and squeezed through holes in rotting fence boards.

Sometimes she looked back and, making certain Kolya and Lena weren't lagging behind, rushed on again.

They passed hardly any people. Just once they saw a woman working on her garden plot. And another time two girls called and asked Niusha to play with them.

Niusha answered briefly, "I'm buthy."

The girls left them alone and didn't say anything else.

After climbing over a high fence, they found themselves in a tiny yard, where a rooster and two hens were roosting in a rubbish heap. A scraggly cat jumped off a shed roof and ran away. They faced the back wall of a one-story brick house. Niusha looked around. There was no one. Only the rooster was striding haughtily atop the rubbish heap, and the hens were pecking unhurriedly at the grass. Niusha bent forward and lifted some boards, which were covering a little window.

"Climb in!" she said. "No one will bother you here. It'h quiet. Wait here till Lyotha comth."

Kolya climbed in first. The cellar seemed shallow. A little box had been placed under the window to make it easier to climb in and out. Kolya called to Lena, and she crawled in on her hands and knees.

Niusha poked her head through the window immediately after.

"Well?" she asked.

"Everything's just fine," Kolya answered.

Her head disappeared, and they heard the sound of sliding boards.

When Kolya's eyes became accustomed to the semidarkness, he noticed a dusty stone floor, stone walls, and a door with rusty hinges, which probably hadn't been opened for a long time. He could make out a pile of straw in a corner and several small boxes piled against the walls.

"We'll get along nicely here, Lena," he said. "You probably want to sleep, don't you?"

"Yes." Lena sat down on a box. "My feet are awfully sore."

Kolya trampled down the straw energetically, fixing a bed for Lena. "Lie down. Close your eyes and think of something nice. Remember Grandfather and our cottage and the lake. . . ."

"Can't we go home?" asked Lena.

"Home? Here, I'll make you a pillow. Then you'll have an honest-to-goodness bed. When you lie down, I'll cover you with straw. It's nice and dry. A little dusty, of course. But it doesn't take long to shake off dust."

"Kolya, why can't we go home?" Lena persisted.

"Home?" Kolya went over to Lena and sat down on a box beside her. "We can't go home. It isn't safe there."

Lena was silent. She lowered her head. Kolya couldn't see her face, but he put his arm around her affectionately.

"You are very tired," he said kindly. "Lie down and go to sleep. I can't tell you why we are being chased just yet, but we must escape. We have to run and hide, but it won't always be that way. It will be different pretty soon. Everything will be good again. Wonderfully good. Better than it's ever been. Meanwhile, don't ask me any more about it. All right?"

"All right," Lena replied sadly. "I'll go to sleep."

She lay down. Kolya covered her with straw and sat beside her. She fell asleep almost immediately, breathing peacefully and evenly.

Hens clucked softly outside. People walked by somewhere in the distance. The sound of their voices was just barely audible, and Kolya couldn't make out their words. It became quiet again. Only a fly buzzed monotonously.

What will we do? What will we do? Kolya repeated to himself. He thought and thought but couldn't supply an answer. Doctor Krechetov was the only person who was easy to find and could help them. But he turned out to be dead, and his sister, the sneaky informer, was almost the undoing of them. Where could they go now? Whom could they turn to? Here in town, or in any village for that matter, there were plenty of people who would be willing to help them hide. But how would they find them? How could they recognize them without making a mistake? What if they should bump into a coward and informer like Krechetova again? They had friends in hiding, but to distinguish a friend from an enemy was impossible. . . .

Kolya suddenly remembered Lyosha, the boy who saved them from being caught and was supposed to come back for them. If he had helped them without knowing anything about them, except that they were being chased by the Germans, that meant he was a friend whom they could depend on.

Now Kolya wondered why he hadn't thought of him before. He recalled the hole under the wall blocked with brushwood on both sides, the prearranged signal with the padlocks, and the girl who wasn't a bit surprised when she found out she had to hide two people. Apparently they had fooled the

Nazis before. Evidently they were brave, loyal children who must be connected with the partisans.

He hadn't even told them who Lena's father was. He simply had said they were being chased and had to get away. Certainly Niusha and Lyosha would help them!

Kolya's heart grew lighter. He didn't even notice that he was falling asleep.

10

Niusha Is a Know-It-All

"Lithen, lithen to me!" someone repeated in Kolya's ear. "You can't thleep any longer. Do you hear?"

Kolya opened his eyes. It was dark in the cellar. A small figure was crouched over him, and a weak hand was shaking his shoulder.

"Who's there?" he asked. "What's happened?"

"It'h me, Niutha. You mutht get up."

Kolya sat up and rubbed his eyes. It was dark outside. He had overslept. His heart sank. "Has Lyosha already come?"

"Lyotha hath been arrethted," the little girl explained excitedly, her words harder to understand than usual because of her alarm. "And they've arrethted the other boyth, too."

"Why did they arrest them? What for?"

"They want to get you, tho they're cathing every boy and girl in the whole town."

"What will we do?" asked Kolya.

"It'h terrible! Terrible!" Niusha whispered.

"They've thtationed tholdierth everywhere. They're looking in everyone'th home, thellar, and thed. It'h terrible! They'll be here any minute now."

Kolya jumped up, ran over to the window, and, standing on a box, poked out his head. Clouds were rushing by high above the earth. Now and then they covered the whole sky. They would part for a moment, letting solitary stars twinkle through or a corner of the moon light up the drowsy earth.

Kolya waited to hear soldier's footsteps or to see figures slinking up on them, but nothing was moving. An empty tin can flashed on the rubbish heap in the moonlight. The iron roof of the shed gleamed. The moon hid behind the clouds again, and everything was plunged into darkness.

Glad of the nighttime tranquility, a cricket chirped in delight. A chicken clucked sleepily, then stopped. This peace seemed false and deceptive to Kolya. He felt danger in the quiet darkness. Somewhere, not far away, the flashlight beams of German officers and police were already probing. And soon—within a half hour or an hour—Lena, Lena whom he must save, would be caught in their light.

Kolya sprang from the box and stood in front of Niusha. Raising her head, Niusha looked at him. When she spoke, there was both curiosity and respect in her voice. "Are you the partithan who blew up the railroad latht week?"

"What railroad?"

"I know! I know all about it. You dynamited it. Lyotha told me."

Good grief! thought Kolya. This girl will credit us with such deeds that the Nazis will raise a general alarm.

He tried to speak quietly and convincingly. "Listen, Niusha, we didn't dynamite any railroad. It's simply that we must get out of town. Do you understand?"

"I know! I know all about it!" Niusha kept nodding. "A partithan mutht never reveal hith identity. Lyotha told me."

That's right, know-it-all. Keep harping on it! Kolya thought to himself angrily. Don't listen to anyone else.

He forced himself to be calm and reasonable. "Think whatever you like," he said, "but get us out of here. Can you do that?"

"Yeth," Niusha replied. "Leth go! They'll thoon be here."

Kolya woke Lena. She had slept well and was in good spirits.

"Are we leaving already?" she asked.

"Yes. It's time to go."

Lena shook the dust off her dress in the darkness and went over to the window. Suddenly Kolya began to hesitate. Niusha is so young, he thought. How can she lead us anywhere?

Niusha must have guessed his doubts. "Are you afraid?" she asked. "Don't be. I know the way Lyotha takth to get to the foreth. He didn't thow me, but I followed him and thaw."

Well, things can't be any worse! Kolya decided silently. He hurriedly gave Lena a helping hand, then climbed out himself.

It seemed like daylight outside after being in the cellar. The light of the moon broke through a cloud, making the house, the shed, and the high fence around the yard fully visible.

Niusha crawled out behind Kolya and quickly slid the boards across the little window. "Follow me!" she ordered briefly.

Once more the endless journey through front yards, back yards, and gardens began. Niusha walked confidently with quick steps. Her manner reassured Kolya. Apparently she knew the way she was leading them pretty well.

The going was tough for Kolya and Lena. First they stumbled into a deep hole. Then they unexpectedly bumped into a fence they hadn't seen in the dark. Soon Kolya had completely lost any idea of the direction they were taking. He had to look down at his feet all the time and grope to climb over fences or search for turns in the path. They stopped frequently, losing sight of Niusha. Kolya was afraid to call her, so he would come to a stop and stand there whistling softly.

They always heard Niusha's tense whisper coming from a most unexpected direction. "Quick! Come on!"

What will we do now? thought Kolya. Everything was turning out fine until we had to leave the cellar. The little girl said that Lyosha often makes trips to the partisans. Maybe we could have reached them with his help. But everything's gone wrong again. The Nazis will bring Lyosha and the other boys to Krechetov's sister for her to identify. Then they'll set them free. Of course, she won't say they aren't the ones they're looking for right away. It will already be too late for us anyway by the time she tells them that. To stay in town and wait till Lyosha is released is impossible. It's too risky. Evidently they've organized a big roundup. To return to town in a day or so isn't practical either. We'd most certainly be arrested. That means we'll have to go back to the forest again without food or friends, not daring to turn to anyone for help. . . .

While mulling things over, Kolya almost bumped into Niusha, who was waiting for them by a shallow ditch. She let Lena pass first. Holding Kolya back for a moment, she whispered in his ear excitedly, "Did the little girl help blow up the railroad, too? I won't tell anyone. Word of honor."

"What railroad?" the enraged Kolya whispered back. "I've told you a hundred times. We haven't blown up anything. We don't even know how to get to the partisans by ourselves."

"I know! I know!" Niusha nodded. "Lyotha told me that a partithan mutht never tell thecreth." She walked ahead quickly, convinced once and for all that Lena and Kolya were partisans of the greatest notoriety and importance.

Muttering to himself, Kolya followed Niusha. Suddenly he felt the ground slip out from under him and just barely managed to grab onto a bush so that he wouldn't fall. He was standing at the top of a slope, which was covered with thick bushes. Below them was the scarcely visible glimmer of a moonlit river.

"Lena!" Kolya called in a whisper.

"I'm here." Lena answered in a whisper also.

Niusha appeared out of the darkness. Kolya couldn't figure out where she had been or what direction she had come from. "Quiet!" she commanded in a scarcely audible whisper. "There are tholdierth nearby. Hold hands."

She grabbed Kolya's hand, and Kolya took hold of Lena's. The three of them began to descend the slope carefully. When one of them stumbled or accidentally kicked a stone, Niusha became paralyzed with fear and repeated in a low whisper, "Quiet, pleathe! Quiet!" Evidently sentries were posted nearby.

Soon Niusha turned straight into a big, thick bush. She pushed some branches aside and, bending over, seemed to be walking into the very depths of its foliage. Kolya bent over, too. He followed her, pulling Lena along behind. They walked stooping down, but their heads brushed against branches now and then just the same. They were in a narrow passageway, which ran through the bushes. The branches overhead were all entangled, forming a long, compact tunnel.

Niusha was absolutely tireless. Lena was already out of breath, and Kolya's legs and back ached. But Niusha walked along as if it were nothing.

Once in a while she stopped to warn them in a soft whisper, "Quiet, pleathe! Quiet!"

Suddenly she halted so abruptly that Kolya almost collided with her. She only made a hissing sound, but from the stiffness of her posture Kolya understood that danger was close at hand. He stayed stooped over, afraid to move, and felt Lena freeze behind him. In front of him, Niusha kept quiet and listened. Then he heard a German phrase and a laugh coming from somewhere just above their heads. Raising his eyes, he could barely see a light weakly penetrating the thick foliage.

"Quiet!" Niusha whispered. After waiting a bit longer, she finally moved forward—very, very slowly —so that not even a twig snapped or a leaf rustled.

They went on in this manner, stopping to listen after each step. Niusha began to quicken her pace. Glancing back, Kolya noticed they were leaving the light, which was dimly piercing the bushes, far behind. He felt relieved. The most dangerous part of their journey was over.

Soon the bushes became sparser, and the cloudy sky appeared more and more often over their heads. They were going away from the river. Ducking down, they hurriedly ran across a road and found themselves in a forest. The sky was already brightening a little.

Kolya looked back. In the semidarkness, he could make out the roofs of Zapolsk, where soldiers and secret police were walking the streets, poking flashlights into cellars and sheds and attics, searching apartments, and grabbing children. The whole town was thrown into an uproar just to catch the tired, frightened, little Lena. And here she was in the forest, fooling all those Nazi soldiers. Lena had escaped the mousetrap that was ready to snap down on her.

This Niusha sure is brave, thought Kolya.

Niusha cheerfully explained to him, "Lyotha found the thecret path. He followth it to the woodth all the time. He never thowed me, but I thpied on him." Then she stood on tiptoes. Motioning toward Lena with her head, she whispered excitedly in his ear, "Lyotha thaid young oneth aren't allowed to join the partithanth. Why did they take her? He mutht have lied to me, huh?"

Kolya had almost forgotten that he and Lena were supposed to have blown up a railroad the week before, so at first he didn't even understand what she was talking about. Then he got angry. There was no way he could convince Niusha that he and Lena were not notorious partisans. Suddenly the notion seemed funny. In a way what Niusha thought made sense. For whose sake would Hitler's soldiers stir up a whole town, if not for someone who had, at the very least, blown up a railroad.

He burst out laughing, slapped Niusha on the back, and said, "Don't worry, Niusha. When you grow up a little, they'll take you, too."

Niusha sniffed. "Good-by," she said. "If you ever need me, jutht athk for Niutha Thalova. Everyone on Garden Thtreet knowth me."

She stepped back resolutely and disappeared into the darkness. Kolya watched her and was even a little sorry that he probably would never see her again. She was a really nice girl!

Still, it was dangerous to linger. Kolya took Lena's hand and stepped into the forest with determination. "Let's go," he said. "We have to be as far away from here as possible before daybreak."

11

Rogachov

Going across the front and taking Lena straight to her father would be impossible. Kolya could see that clearly. The nearer they came to the front line, the more patrols there would be blocking roads and the more units there would be stationed in the forests. Only one possibility was left: to find the partisans.

However, there was little hope of that. The partisans had learned to leave no traces behind, noiselessly making their way along invisible paths and hiding in places where no one would venture without knowing the terrain.

Kolya and Lena lay down on the grass under a big birch tree. They had been walking since dawn, stopping to rest only now and then in an attempt to get as far away as possible from Zapolsk. They hadn't eaten anything except berries all day long. A blue sky with slow-moving, white clouds suspended in its endless depths peeked through the birch leaves. It seemed odd that the clouds didn't either fall down to earth or rise up to infinity. Lena looked up at them. When the wind made the leaves rustle, she listened, trying to understand what the birch was talking about. It could very well be that trees know a lot but just can't communicate with people. After all the birch was very, very old. Its hollow was like the smiling mouth of a toothless old man. Imagine the things it must have seen in its day!

"Do you want me to pick some more bilberries?" asked Kolya.

"No, never mind. Tell me about Rogachov, the man someone was singing about on the boat."

Kolya was embarrassed. He looked at Lena. No, she must have said that by chance. She didn't suspect anything.

"He is a famous Soviet general," said Kolya, "who commanded the regiments that defended Moscow. Then he and his division fought near Stalingrad, where there were millions of Nazis. Rogachov's regiments swooped down on them like a storm cloud. Rogachov, himself, led them. He had a saber in his hand and wore a black felt cloak over his shoulders. When the Germans saw him, they cried out in fear and fell. He chopped them all down.

'Aha!' he said. 'You kill and torture our people, so here—take that!'"

Kolya continued his story with mounting enthusiasm. "Afterwards our most important generals had a meeting and called for Rogachov. They pinned the Gold Star on his chest and put the whole Army under his command. He jumped on his horse again and cried out, 'Follow me!' Then he went to the big, wide Dnieper River. The Nazis didn't think our men would cross it, but Rogachov whipped his horse and rushed forward with his felt cloak flowing in the wind. The Army followed him, of course, one after another. They're splendid warriors! How their horses leaped into the Dnieper! The Nazis were transporting tanks, artillery, machine guns, and mortar, but Rogachov and his men swam across just the same. When their horses reached the other bank, Rogachov's men took out their sabers. The Nazis ran away again, screaming with fear. They abandoned their tanks and guns. Many of them raised their arms and begged, 'Have mercy on us, General Rogachov.' 'Did you have mercy on our men?' Rogachov asked. 'Did you have mercy on Doctor Krechetov? Or my daughter when she was roaming the forests, cold and hungry. . . .'"

Kolya stopped and gave Lena a frightened look.

She was gazing through the birch trees into the blue sky with its clouds drifting no one knows where.

"And does Rogachov have a daughter?" she asked.

"I don't know," Kolya answered. "I was only using that as an example."

"Well, yes," said Lena. "Of course. Where is he now?"

"Not far away. After he drove the Nazis from the Dnieper, the Government called for him. He was told, 'You are a brave general, Rogachov. There is still land beyond the Dnieper, however, where people are tormented by Hitler's men.' 'So there is,' General Rogachov answered. 'That will soon be taken care of, comrades!' And he jumped on his horse again. His men fell in behind him. 'Forward!' Rogachov ordered. Now people say he is nearby. They say the Nazis are on the run again, screaming with fear and leaving their tanks and guns behind."

Kolya lashed a switch he had picked up against a tree stump with all his might. Lena lay motionless as before, looking at the sky through the foliage. The switch snapped, and Kolya flung the broken piece aside. He got so carried away talking about Rogachov that he couldn't calm down. They were both silent for a long time.

Lena broke the silence. "My father was a soldier, too. Grandfather told me he was a schoolteacher, but I remember he was a soldier—a colonel. He might have been a teacher too, of course, but Mama always said he was a colonel. Everyone always called him that. Only he wasn't like General Rogachov. He didn't have a saber. He was tall. . . ." Lena's voice trailed off. "But he didn't have a saber. I'm quite sure of it," she said with conviction.

Kolya looked at her. No, she hadn't guessed a thing. "Lena, are you very hungry? Out with it, if you are. We can eat some more bilberries."

"No, thanks," Lena answered.

Kolya jumped up. "You know what? I'll go into the village and buy some bread. You won't be afraid to stay here alone, will you? I'll be back in two hours. Three at the most."

"No," Lena replied, "I won't be afraid. Do you have enough money?"

"I think so. Just don't go off anywhere. And if you get scared, go out onto the road. Sit down alongside it and wait for me."

He left with an aching heart. How sluggish Lena had become! She had never been like that before. What if he wasn't able to bring her to her father? No, he mustn't even think that way, although she clearly was getting weak. After all they had gone probably a hundred and fifty versts without having even one really good rest. And they had eaten hardly anything these last few days. He was very tired too, but he considered himself almost grown-up. Today he could still buy some bread for them, but tomorrow he probably wouldn't have any money left. What would he do then? Where were the partisans?

Lost in thought, he walked down the road that led to the village.

12

Alone in the Forest

Left alone, Lena lay quietly for a long while. She thought of the fresh fish soup and fried mushrooms Grandfather used to make. That memory didn't make things any easier. On the contrary, she wanted something to eat more than ever. She thought of her mother and father. Mama used to wake her up every morning. It felt good to sleep. She didn't want to get up, but Mama's voice was kind and pleasant. Lena smiled and opened her eyes. . . .

In the evening Lena used to sit in Mama's lap as the lamp shone and gray shadows gathered in the corners of the room. It was dark outside, but she wasn't afraid as long as her mother was near. The thought that someone might be hidden in the darkness didn't bother her at all. . . .

When Papa and Mama would go to the theater, Mama always took a long time getting dressed. Grumbling and out of sorts, Papa would claim they were already late, but not too angrily. . . .

Generally speaking, life was good back then. There had been troubles, of course, but they hadn't been very serious. How nice if it could be like that again, even for a little while!

Lena grew sad and didn't even notice she was crying. She cried and cried, but her tears didn't make things any better. Just the opposite!

The wind died down, and the trees stopped moving. It was so quiet all around that Lena became frightened. She heard a rustling noise in the silence, so she got up and paced back and forth, looking behind the trunk of the birch over and over again. No one was there. The next time she walked by the tree, she turned round abruptly. There wasn't anyone behind her either. She sat down on a stump.

There's nothing to be afraid of! she thought. What could be in the forest? Absolutely nothing.

She stood on one foot, put one hand on her hip, and imagined she was a general inspecting with an eagle eye the officers standing around. "Well, are you ready for battle?" she asked them. "Ready? Well, very good. My officers have informed me that a girl by the name of Lena is living in the forest. The Nazis are after her. It is urgent that we save her. Follow me!"

She raised a stick as if it were a saber and dashed

forward. "Quick! Cut them down!" she shouted.

Then she switched roles and pretended to be a Nazi. "Oh, please don't touch us. We'll go away," she screamed plaintively.

"Go away?" asked the so-called general, leaning on her stick saber. "Oh, you so-and-sos!" Then the general said to one of her officers, "Take some hot pancakes with honey syrup, roast chicken, creamed cottage cheese, and a lump of lard to Lena."

Lena became herself and bowed politely in a grown-up manner to the general as if she had just eaten her fill. "Hello, general!" she said. "Thank you very much. I am quite all right now. You know, general, my cousin Kolya wants to be an Army officer."

"Is he brave?" the general asked.

"Terribly brave," Lena answered.

"Then appoint him my chief officer!" the general commanded.

Lena froze. She heard a strange rumbling sound. It came closer and closer. The forest seemed to be loudly and angrily buzzing. High above the tree-tops big, heavy airplanes rushed over Lena and the old birch tree. Enormous, fast, and roaring angrily, they flew side by side. Red stars were painted on their wings.

If she could only shout to them to take her with them. She stood looking into the sky, shaking all over with excitement. Maybe they would notice her and pick her up. Rescues always happened that way in stories. But the airplanes passed by, and the sky became clear and empty again. Their roaring sounded farther and farther away, and finally it faded. Once again the rustling birch leaves could be heard.

Lena lay down on the grass. She felt very tired again. She looked at the birch with its curved trunk and its hollow that resembled an open mouth. All at once she felt very weak. Branches and leaves swam before her eyes. Her thoughts were confused. Finally she fell asleep.

When she awoke, she was shaking from the cold. The sun was shining brightly, but the grass was wet with dew. When Lena discovered she had slept the whole night, her heart sank.

"Kolya!" she shouted. "Kolya!"

No one answered.

Well, maybe he stayed too late in the village. He must not have been able to find his way back at night, she thought, trying to be calm. Nothing could have happened. Pretty soon Kolya will be here and everything will be all right.

She lay down again, a slight shiver running through her body. The grass rustled. She gave a start and jumped up. A field mouse, standing on its hind legs, looked at her fearfully.

"Please, don't scare me." Lena spoke in a reasonable tone of voice. "After all I know you are a very ordinary mouse who wishes me no harm."

The mouse darted into the grass and disappeared. Lena sat down again, but the shivering didn't stop.

"Well, what's the matter?" she asked. "Why doesn't he come?"

Lena imagined what would happen to her if she were left all alone, and she became so terrified that she began calling frantically for Kolya. Nobody answered, so she stopped. She remembered that Kolya told her to go out onto the road if she got scared. That was just the way she felt—scared—so she decided to follow his advice. Now that she knew what she must do, she felt better. When she got up she staggered weakly, but she walked ahead just the same.

Soon the forest got thinner. The road wasn't far off, for Lena could hear the sound of passing vehicles. It came into view. The sun's rays got warmer and warmer. She stopped shivering. After coming out onto the road, she looked first in one direction,

then in the other. It was deserted. Lena sat down
and waited.

Every now and then she saw somebody in the
distance. Each time she thought it was Kolya. When
the person came nearer, it would turn out to be a
woman or an old man. It was terrible to be without
Kolya. If he were around, he would be sure to think
of something. They would at least be able to talk
with one another. Of course, she wouldn't tell him
she was hungry and tired, but she would know just
the same that he felt sorry for her. That would make
her feel better.

Time passed. The sun rose high in the sky, but
still there was no sign of Kolya.

13

The Convoy of Prisoners

More people appeared in the distance. This time they were in a large group, so Kolya couldn't be among them. He always tried to avoid people. Lena didn't examine the crowd walking down the road until it came closer. Then she could see that soldiers with submachine guns were walking on both sides. In the middle were men and women, adolescents and middle-aged people, carrying little bundles.

Ivan Ignatyevich Solomin and his grandchildren had lived in solitude. Nevertheless, Lena had grown up in territory occupied by Hitler's soldiers, and she didn't need anyone to explain to her the nature of the strange caravan coming down the road. She knew the soldiers were driving people away from their homes into Germany, where they would have to work for the Nazis. Elderly men and women, shaking from old age, and little children were walking along the side of the road.

When the convoy came nearer, Lena could hear
and see everything.

The soldiers walked with measured steps, not
paying any attention to the screams and words of
the weeping people, who were saying good-by to
one another.

"Mama! Mama!" a young woman walking in the
convoy shouted to an old lady, who was dragging
a three- or four-year-old little boy along by the
hand. "Make sure Volodka doesn't fall into the well,
and tell him to remember his mother. Do you hear
me, Mama? And if Father returns, tell him they
took me away. Do you hear, Mama? Be sure to
tell him."

Apparently the old lady was completely deaf.
Even a person with good hearing would have had
difficulty making anything out of the shouts and
conversations that were continually interrupting one
another. But the old lady didn't have to hear. She
understood very well what her daughter must be
talking about just before leaving for a foreign country as a prisoner.

"Yes, yes," she repeated. "I hear, Niurochka. I
hear. I'll take care of everything."

"Grandpa," shouted a boy, who was about fourteen years old, "if Dad comes home, tell him to go to Germany to rescue me! I'll be waiting for him. Do you hear, Grandpa?"

"I hear you," the old man answered. "If he comes home, he'll go get you."

A young girl, lame in one leg, hobbled down the side of the road yelling parting words to a friend, who was walking in the convoy. How her friend must have envied her for being lame and consequently useless to the Germans as a prisoner!

Holding hands, a mother and daughter were walking in the convoy as a younger girl ran down the side of the road.

"You come back," she called to her sister and mother. "Come back or I'll die here all alone!"

"Don't worry. We'll be back," her mother shouted, wondering to herself all the while how she could ever return. "Maybe some kindhearted people will help you out while we're gone."

The convoy escorts walked along without hurrying. They looked around indifferently and paid about as much attention to the tears and pleas as a horse pays to the monotonous buzzing of flies. As lazily as a horse flicks its tail, they waved their submachine guns at any person who came too close.

Taken aback, Lena looked at the people who were parting—most likely, forever—those who were being driven into enemy captivity and those who would remain behind without their loved ones.

Suddenly she heard her name called. "Lena!"

She didn't even turn around, she was so certain that the shout couldn't have anything to do with her. But a loud, excited voice kept repeating, "Lena! Lena!" Finally she turned because the voice seemed oddly familiar.

When Lena swung round, she almost screamed. Kolya, her Kolya, was walking in the convoy chained to one of the armed soldiers. Small and pitiful, he smiled at her as he walked along.

"Kolya!" Lena shouted, running up to him. Without even looking, the soldier lazily hit her in the shoulder with his gun butt. She jumped back and almost fell into the ditch, but immediately started after Kolya again.

"Kolya," she shouted, "Kolya, are you all right? What are you doing?"

"They arrested me on the street in the village. Don't worry, Lena!"

He smiled and tried very hard to reassure her, to show her things weren't so terrible, but big tears were running down his smiling face, one after another. "Lena," he called, "listen closely. It's very important! Ask me to repeat if you don't understand. First of all, you must be very hungry. Go to Selishchye Village. I left some bread there for you at old man Bugayev's. He's an honest old man and is sure to give it to you. Do you understand?"

"Mama! Mama!" shouted a little boy, running almost parallel with Lena. "Mama, address your letters to the Sinyavins. They'll send them to me. I'm going away somewhere, Mama!"

"I hear. I hear," a deaf old man, who probably didn't hear anything, shouted to someone.

"Lena, listen carefully. This is very serious. I must tell you a secret, a terribly important secret," said Kolya, feeling confident that the German-speaking soldier to whom he was chained couldn't understand Russian. "Do you hear me, Lena?"

"Yes, yes, Kolya. I understand."

"Now listen carefully. You are the daughter of that very same man we talked about yesterday."

"What man? Who?"

"Just don't say his last name! I'll explain to you. The man someone was singing about when we were on the boat. The one you asked me about. Just don't say his last name. Do you understand who I mean?"

"Grandma!" shouted a boy, who was walking beside Kolya. "Grandma, if I see Mama there, I'll have a chat with her. You just wait for us to come home."

"Yes, yes," the old woman running alongside Lena answered. "I'll wait. I'll wait."

"I don't understand a thing," Lena shouted. "You know my father was a schoolteacher."

"No, no. Grandfather made that up so that you wouldn't give us away. You know what I mean? Be careful and keep quiet about it."

"Tell the girls not to forget me," the young girl shouted to her lame friend.

"Don't worry. We'll never forget you!" answered her friend.

"Kolya, Kolya, I'm scared! Dear Kolya, find some way to escape!" Lena was crying as hard as she could, wiping away the tears with her fist.

"I'll try, but don't depend on it. Lena, remember—go to old man Bugayev. You can trust him. He'll take you back to Grandfather."

The noise evidently was annoying the officer walking in front of the group. Turning to the soldiers, he shouted a command. They jerked up their guns. Several soldiers unlocked their own ends of the chains and went over to the people who were running after the convoy. Old people, boys and

girls, mothers and fathers, grandmothers and grand-
fathers, and sons and daughters kept screaming and
trying to reach their loved ones, whom they were
seeing for the last time.

The soldiers raised their guns and aimed at the
crowd. People dashed aside. Bursts of gunfire broke
out. Suddenly the soldiers fell. They lay sprawled
on the ground next to their guns, which had dropped
out of their hands. Shots kept pelting the area. The
commanding officer turned, intending to shout something, but reeled, then fell. His cap flew off his head
and rolled down the road.

"Get down!" someone shouted. Lena caught sight
of a short young man in a black satin shirt standing
by a tree at the side of the road. "Get down!" he
continued to shout. "Oh, what simpletons! Get down
or you'll get hit."

Lena was so confused and surprised that she
wasn't even frightened. She stood without moving.
An old woman, evidently experienced in battle tac-
tics, gave her such a hard push that she fell into
the ditch. Several people immediately jumped over
her. She saw only their shoes.

Submachine guns started to rattle. Grenades ex-
ploded. A woman screamed.

Then the short young man leaned over the ditch

and said, "You can come out now, citizens! Those who lived by the sword have died by the sword."

Everything happened so suddenly that Lena needed some time to come to her senses. Only when Kolya, happy and beaming, ran over to her, grabbed her by the shoulder, and gave her a big kiss, did she let out a sob and wipe her nose with her hand.

"Dear Kolya!" she said through another big sob.

The bodies of those same indifferent soldiers, who had listened to the cries and tears of their prisoners so coldly and nonchalantly, now lay on the road. The jaunty, grand commanding officer lay facedown. His appearance was far from magnificent. The freed people crowded onto the road in confusion, crying or smiling or simply looking around in amazement.

Jumping up again, the young man shouted, "Step lively! Step lively! Follow me!"

Then an elderly man with a moustache asked in a businesslike manner, "Did you collect their guns?"

"Yes," the partisans answered.

"Sidorenko will cover us. Wait here an hour, Sidorenko. Got it?"

"Got it," he answered.

Everybody—women, children, and old people— quickly went into the forest, following the young man, who walked ahead of them to show the way.

Now and then he glanced back and shouted, "Faster! Faster, comrades! Maybe that's the way you walked when the Nazis were leading you, but walking along like a sick fly just won't do here!"

He shouted angrily, then suddenly broke into a loud, merry laugh. The laughter was not caused by anything funny. He was simply happy to have succeeded in freeing so many people.

14

The Quarrel

At first they walked along a wide, clearly marked forest path. They went fast. The partisans kept hurrying anyone who lagged behind. Parents and children, husbands and wives, brothers and sisters who had been prepared for a long, possibly even final, separation were as happy as if they had just found one another again. Some talked on and on, recalling every detail of their rescue. Others did just the opposite and looked silently at each other as though they couldn't see enough.

The farther they went, the thicker the forest became. The path, which had already narrowed and was half overgrown with grass, twisted among closely spaced trees. They walked single file. In about an hour, fifty people separated from the main group and went in another direction. The freed prisoners had to spread out at several different points. In another hour, a second party of people left them.

Now only three old women, two old men, and the lame girl were walking with Lena and Kolya. The same merry young man who had led them from the beginning was in command. He hurried his party along by yelling at them occasionally and was very angry that they moved so slowly.

The lame girl, hobbling ahead, turned out to be a pretty good walker. The three old women walked behind her, and the two old men followed. Kolya and Lena trailed along behind all the rest.

Everybody was walking rather slowly, but Lena trudged along even slower than the others and lagged behind constantly. She didn't pay any attention either to the scolding of their guide or to Kolya's persuasions.

"We're falling behind," he said. "Walk faster."

"I can't," Lena answered dejectedly, slowing down even more, as though on purpose.

"Don't lag behi-i-nd," their guide shouted cheerfully. "Hurry up!"

The lame girl quickened her pace, and the old people, following her example, took heart and hurried after her. Their guide's words didn't impress Lena in the least. She plodded along, and with each step she dropped farther and farther behind. Kolya grabbed her hand.

"For goodness sake! Let's catch up to them, or we'll get lost!"

Lena pulled back her hand irritably. "Let us! You can go chase them, but I won't."

Their guide had disappeared around a bend in the path. The lame girl hobbled after him energetically. Lena dragged along as she had been doing, without paying any attention to the fact that the distance between her and the others was growing greater and greater. Her frowning face reflected her bad mood.

"I want to eat," she declared suddenly.

Kolya had never heard her speak in such a malicious, wayward tone of voice.

"You must have eaten in the village. Why didn't you bring some bread for me?"

Kolya was quite taken aback. He couldn't believe it was Lena talking to him. "You know I left some bread for you in the village," he muttered. "I don't understand how you can talk like that!"

Lena shrugged. The old ladies had already disappeared around the bend. Only the backs of the two old men could be seen up ahead. "Yes," she whined spitefully, "no doubt you ate and slept in a nice house. But I slept in the forest. Do you think that's fun? Huh?"

Her words were so ridiculous, her tone of voice so unlike her, that Kolya didn't even get angry. "Stop sulking, Lena," he said lightheartedly. "Do you want me to tell you a story? Would you like to hear about General Rogachov?"

"No!" Lena said sharply. "What do I care about him?"

"Lena!" Kolya exclaimed.

"Besides, besides," continued Lena, stumbling over her words hurriedly, "you left me for a whole night alone in the forest! I might have been eaten up by wolves there. Besides, besides, bears could have almost killed me. Of course, it doesn't matter to you what happens to me!"

"Don't you dare talk like that," replied Kolya, trying to control himself. "Do you understand?"

But Lena couldn't stop. She was beside herself. "I will so dare," she said. "I want to and I dare! Please go away. It makes no difference. I don't want to be with you anyway. I'm going to sit down here, and I'm not going to get up. You'd just as soon I'd die of hunger. So there!"

She sat on a stump and turned away from Kolya. Kolya, his face red with anger, stood in front of her. He thrust his hands into his pockets and doubled them into fists. "If you keep talking like that," he said slowly and distinctly, "I *will* go away."

"Go away then! Well, why don't you?"

"I will!" Kolya clenched his teeth so tightly that he could hardly speak.

"No, you won't, because you're a coward. You're afraid that Grandfather will punish you for leaving me, you cowardly little boy!"

"That does it!" Kolya whispered.

"You're bragging," Lena continued. "You don't dare go away. Do you think I need you? I don't need you at all."

Kolya turned around sharply and, without saying another word, ran off the path straight into the forest. He was choking with rage. He ran without watching where he was going. Picking up a stick that was lying in his way, he banged it against the side of a tree so hard that it shattered into pieces. The action helped calm him down a little. Then he picked up another big stick and began switching the tops of some ferns growing among the trees.

The battered ferns fell to the ground. Kolya felt a little better. He paused for breath. The initial strength of his seething rage left him. "Well, what if she is younger?" he asked, keeping time to his words with a wave of the stick. "What of it? She's only five years younger."

The stick broke. Kolya threw what was left of it away and, thrusting his hands into his pockets, started walking back and forth.

"She's seven years old," he said, fiercely stomping on the grass. "That's pretty old. By the time a person is seven, he knows how to read and write. And should be able to reason and understand. . . . Why not just say to Rogachov, 'I wanted to bring your daughter to you, but she has such a nasty temper it was impossible'?"

He walked slower and slower and finally stopped, leaning against a tree. Bending over, he broke off a blade of grass and began to bite off pieces and spit them out.

Let's put it this way. She really is awfully young, he thought, but what is the matter with her? She's never been like this.

Then he remembered not the Lena he left a few minutes ago, sulky and spiteful, but the Lena he knew before, the cheerful little girl who lived at the forest hideaway, the fancier of raspberries and birch buds, the trusting and obedient companion of all his adventures. He sucked in his stomach.

What foolishness! he thought. I wonder what she

makes of all this. A girl seven years old has her own
ideas about things. Of course, he reasoned, seven
isn't twelve. A twelve-year-old is almost grown up.
He knows history and geography and can work.
Sometimes he can even advise grown-ups. But, of
course, a seven-year-old is still a child. Besides she's
tired. She's eaten almost nothing for two days. She's
upset. A fellow twelve years old has a big reserve
of energy and can endure more, but it's hard for a
seven-year-old. I may not be able to reason with
her, but I must hand her over to the partisans.

After hesitating a moment, he turned and walked
back unhurriedly. As he walked, he slackened his
pace on purpose, although he really wanted to run.
She's probably caught up to the others a long time
ago and is walking with the old people. I'll just take
her to the camp, then go back to Grandfather. He
and I will spend our lives together. Just the two
of us.

Kolya found the path and stopped. Lena was in
the same place he had left her, only she was lying
on the grass doubled up in a little ball.

He went over to her noiselessly and looked at her
face. Her eyes were shut, but tears were streaming
out from under her lowered lids, falling onto the
grass, one after another. Her face was fiery red, and

her whole body from her head to her little, tucked-in feet was quivering. A terrible thought flashed across Kolya's mind. He stooped down and put his hand on Lena's forehead. Her head was so hot that there was no doubt. Lena was sick—seriously, dangerously sick.

She opened her eyes and looked at him. "Don't bother with me," she sobbed. "It's better for Papa not to know about me," she sobbed again, "just as if I weren't alive."

Kolya put his hands under her knees and shoulders and lifted her up. "I don't know," he said grimly, "if you can ever forgive me for being such a fool, but I will never forgive myself."

15

The Storm

Carrying Lena was difficult. Kolya was already panting after just a few steps. Only then did he realize how much strength he had lost in the last few days. He decided to go slower and make frequent rest stops.

Lena dozed with her arms clasped around his neck. She was so helpless and miserable that when Kolya remembered their recent quarrel, he was seized with shame and repentence.

He made his way by walking fifty steps, sitting on a tree stump or a fallen tree to rest one or two minutes, then repeating the procedure all over again. After going one thousand steps, he decided to give himself a longer rest.

Soon he came across an unexpected complication. The path forked into two different directions. Both new paths were barely noticeable and overgrown with grass. Deciding which one the party of freed prisoners had taken was completely impossible.

Kolya set Lena down under a tree and began to look the grass over carefully, hoping to find some kind of trace. But the grass on both paths looked slightly crushed as though someone had walked on it, so there was just as much reason for choosing one as the other.

To stay there and wait until someone came back for them would be unthinkable. In all the commotion the guide might not notice the children were missing, or he might suppose they had gone with one of the parties that had separated from the group. After thinking the situation over for a while, Kolya decided to take a gamble and choose a path at random.

"Eventually both paths must wind up in the deepest part of the forest," he reasoned, "and I doubt they branch off very far from one another. Most likely they both lead to the partisan camp."

He took Lena in his arms and started measuring off fifty steps again. After five hundred steps, he had to rest for about ten minutes. His back was breaking, and his hands had gone numb. His next long rest came after three hundred steps. In another two hundred, Kolya felt that he could no longer go on.

Lena dozed in his arms. She opened her eyes for a second when Kolya put her down on the grass but went right to sleep again. Kolya gathered some grass to make her a pillow. He stuck a leafy branch in the ground to keep the sun out of her eyes and covered her with his jacket. Lena slept peacefully. Kolya decided he could sleep a bit, too. He felt he must. The other night, locked in the commandant's office, he hadn't slept a wink. He lay down right on the path so that the partisans would be sure to notice him if they made a search. As soon as he put his head down on a mound of grass, he fell asleep.

While Kolya was asleep, the partisans were indeed looking for him, but they weren't looking in the right place. The children's disappearance wasn't observed right away. It was noticed only when the party settled down to rest.

Their guide dug into a hole, which was covered with leaves, took out some canned food and biscuits, made a head count, and said in alarm, "Look here, there were two more. A little boy and girl!"

There was an immediate strict questioning of the lame girl, the three old women, and the two old men. But not one of them could remember anything. They were even doubtful about whether or not there really had been a little girl and boy. In the end they decided that if there had been, they had gone with another party. After feeding his group and suggesting they rest for an hour or so, the guide decided to retrace their route and look for the laggers, just to be on the safe side. He went to the place where the last group had separated but didn't discover anyone. The thought that the children could have taken the other path didn't occur to him.

Consequently, no one disturbed them. Kolya didn't wake till evening.

He awoke then because bright streaks of lightning were flashing across the sky and it was thundering. He jumped up. It was already quite dark. Trees, bent by the blowing wind, were waving their branches. The first drops of rain were falling on the ground. Kolya ran over to Lena. She was still asleep. He stooped over her.

"Lena," he said, "it's starting to rain. We must go."

"All right," she answered indifferently. "Right away. I'll rest for just a minute. Then we'll go."

If she had objected and said she couldn't go, or complained, he would have felt better. But this indifference, this complete lack of interest, indicated more than tears and grumbling that she was sick.

He lifted her. She stood up and staggered, but he held her up. A strange feeling came over him. Time was passing, and days were turning into nights. The Red Army, commanded by General Rogachov, was fighting. All this while he and Lena had been walking and would continue to walk in the dark forest, stumbling from weariness and yet not daring to stop. Old birches stretched out their long branches. The wind howled through the leafy treetops. It seemed to Kolya that the forest was endless, that it would go on forever and ever, and that he and Lena were destined to toil eternally along this interminable path.

He kept his arms around Lena to hold her up. She walked one step at a time. Her head hung down on her chest, and she was talking softly and unintelligibly.

"What did you say?" Kolya asked.

She didn't hear his question and spoke hurriedly again. It was impossible to understand a word, her mumbling was so incoherent.

"Lena," Kolya shouted. "Little Lena, are you asleep?" He knew very well that she was delirious. "Lena, wake up!"

She was silent for a moment, then began to speak

in another tone. She seemed to be herself again. "You know, Kolya, I don't feel very well. And you know what I think? That maybe the General Rogachov someone was singing about on the boat—you remember?—that maybe he's my father. Of course Father is a colonel and teacher, but that's what I think anyway."

However much Kolya was afraid of dangerous meetings, he would have entered any village he came upon without hesitation. Anything would be better than this dark forest and Lena's senseless mumbling. For all he knew her sickness might be serious. Maybe Lena would die.

"Come to your senses," he said. "What are you talking about? You know Rogachov is your father. I told you so myself."

"Yes, yes, of course, I know. I know all that. . . ."

"Lena! Little Lena!" Kolya shook her.

She looked at him with uncomprehending eyes.

Rain gushed down in buckets. Water, forcing itself through the foliage in spurts, pelted the ground. The earth was wet through in an instant, and streams poured between trees. Kolya picked Lena up in his arms. He adjusted his jacket with difficulty so that it would cover Lena to give her a little protection from the rain. His boots were already filled with dirt and leaves after a few steps. The soles were slipping up and down. Going on became unbearably difficult. Lightning flashed. Tree branches waved. Torrents of water rushed noiselessly to earth. Ankle-deep in water, Kolya made his way, keeping his footing only with great effort.

"Never mind. Never mind," he said, holding Lena tight. "It's not so bad, is it? It can't rain forever, you know. It will rain for a little while, then stop."

Kolya sloshed along and, growing weak, leaned against a birch trunk. He kept trying to cover Lena better with his jacket to protect her from the rain. From under the jacket Lena spoke in a feeble, tired voice.

"Did you say something?" Kolya asked.

"Put me down. I'm too heavy. You can come back to get me tomorrow."

"Sh-h-h! Be quiet," Kolya persuaded her. "You mustn't speak. You'll catch cold."

Flashes of lightning illuminated the forest. Kolya noticed a hut made of fir branches beside the path. Slipping and almost falling into the mud, he made his way to the hut. Once inside, streams of water came down a little less forcefully, but drops never stopped trickling through the needles onto Kolya's head, shoulders, and neck. Bending over Lena, Kolya tried to protect her from falling drops. He listened.

Lena spoke again. "Aren't you going away? I don't know what came over me. I never meant it. You're probably angry, aren't you?"

"Be quiet. My goodness, you're still talking about that! Let's forget we quarreled. Just as though it never happened."

"Kolya, don't go away!" Lena repeated. "I'm afraid that you're angry with me."

"Sh-h-h! You mustn't open your mouth, or you'll catch cold."

The wind bent enormous trees, and rolling peals of thunder boomed from the sky. The wind swooped down on the hut. At first it tore away one branch. Then it loosened another, ripped it off, and tossed it aside while it was loosening a third. Like an infuriated giant, the wind tugged branches, one after another, away from the hut, threw them to the ground and trampled them underfoot. Then it rushed on—to shake trees, chase clouds, and howl and whistle, leaving only the skeleton of a hut beside the path. Exposed to the lashing, slanting streams of rain, Kolya and Lena sat huddled against one another under a few remaining bare branches, which were tied together.

Lightning flashed again. Thunder pealed somewhere far in the distance. Then the rain no longer beat down in continuous streams. Instead, soft drops made a monotonous noise on the leaves. Everything was plunged into pitch-black darkness.

Suddenly there appeared in the dark a shining dot of light. It looked as though it were swaying to and fro. Slowly, but surely, it came closer. Kolya kept watching it, unable to tear his eyes away. He was so weak that he couldn't even scream. By now he could see that it was a storm lantern, which was moving toward them. Its illumination showed slowly advancing mud-covered boots and a little section of the path that had been washed away by the rain.

Swaying evenly, the storm lantern continued to move forward. The boots sloshed along steadily in the mud. All of a sudden the lantern stopped and was raised. Its light revealed a tarpaulin hood and an elderly face with a fluffy, gray moustache.

"Good grief!" exclaimed the man holding the lantern. "There's someone here!"

A tall, thin woman stepped out of the darkness into the circle of light. "Well, there certainly is," she said. "It's a little boy and girl."

Soaking wet, shaking, and holding Lena close, Kolya sat there looking tensely and fearfully at the people bent over them.

"Well, young man, who are you and how did you happen to come here?" asked the man.

"This is my cousin," replied Kolya. "She's sick."

The moustache began to move. "Well, well, let's have a look. . . . You take the girl, Aleksandra Petrovna. It looks like you can't walk either, young man. Well, just climb onto my back and make yourself at home there."

The lantern swayed, its unsteady light falling on trees, puddles, and wet grass, which rose out of the water. After climbing piggyback style onto the man's back, Kolya laid his head on his shoulder.

Trees appeared and disappeared in the darkness. To Kolya, they seemed to be first the old men walking in the Nazis' prisoner convoy, then the partisans jumping out of the forest. Kolya started now and then, but for some reason it seemed to him that now everything would be all right.

16

After the Storm

Kolya saw a dark village street and heard the muted barking of a dog and the creaking of a door as if in a dream. He saw a brightly lighted cottage. A boy came forward to meet them, then bustled around making a bed. Staggering, Kolya went over to the bench that was to be his bed, pulled up the blanket, and immediately fell asleep. He dreamed of his home in the forest, of Grandfather sitting on the little porch, and of cheeping baby chicks squeezing under their mother's wings.

He awoke in a room filled with sunshine. For some time he could not remember what had happened and how he came to be there.

A boy, whom Kolya vaguely remembered having seen when he arrived, was seated at a table writing, his tongue sticking out the side of his mouth. His work didn't come easily. He dipped his pen into the inkwell, sighed, looked it over, then carefully traced thin lines. Although he displayed great patience and conscientiousness, his fingers and even his ear and nose were all inky. On a bench at the other end of the table sat a stubbed-tail fox terrier with an ear that had been slightly torn in a savage fight, a one-eyed yellow cat that seemed to be winking at everything and grinning at a private joke, and a black raven that held its head as though a strong, stiff collar were keeping its neck propped up.

The boy thought awhile; then, looking at the fox terrier and raven, he asked, "Does *somersault* have a *u* in it?"

The dog gave a yelp, and the raven cocked its head to the side and screamed, "Raven, little raven!"

"Idiots!" exclaimed the irritated boy. "It's no use asking you anything, but I have to anyway. Who else is there to ask?"

Kolya couldn't contain himself any longer and burst out laughing. The fox terrier turned toward him, raised his ear so that it stuck out like a signal flag, and barked. The cat looked at Kolya and winked. Showing off more than usual, the raven twirled its head around and shifted from one leg to another.

The boy carefully put his fountain pen into the inkwell and ran his hand over his face, apparently hoping to wipe the stain off his nose. Instead, he left a wide, purple stripe on his cheek. Since he couldn't see the stripe, he considered everything to be in order.

"Are you awake?" he asked. "Well, hello."

"Where's Lena?" Kolya asked sullenly.

"You mean your cousin? She's at a neighbor's house. Aleksandra Petrovna's. She's sick, you see. She has pneumonia."

Kolya sprang out of bed and hurriedly began to get dressed.

"What're you doing? Do you want to go see her?" asked the boy. "Don't be in such a hurry. Father probably won't let you."

"And just who is your father?" Kolya growled. Lately he had become so used to being on guard against enemies that this unknown father, the boy, and even the fox terrier, cat, and raven seemed suspect to him.

The boy passed his hand through his hair, leaving an even stripe of ink on it, and said quietly and gravely, "Don't bellow at me. There's nothing for you to be angry about. My father, Vasily Georgiyevich Golubkov, is the local feldsher. Yesterday, on his way back from visiting a patient, he found you and your cousin in the forest. He picked you up, because he didn't want you to die there. He carried you on his back for five kilometers and put you up in his own house. Your cousin is at our midwife's, Aleksandra Petrovna's. He did all this despite the fact that it is dangerous on account of the Nazis, who come here and seize anyone suspicious. Do you understand that or not?"

Kolya stopped and thought for a moment, then turned and said, "Don't be angry with me. Let's be friends."

"That's better," said the boy, extending his hand. "What's your name?"

"Kolya. And yours?"

"Mine is Vladik, and the fox terrier is Zhuk. How old are you?"

"Twelve."

"Me too . . . at least, pretty soon I will be. Well, let's go now. Maybe Father will let you see your cousin."

They went out. The village was very small. There were no more than ten houses on either side of the street. A narrow ring of fields, fenced in with stakes, surrounded the village. Beyond them, the forest began. The street was empty. Only lazy dogs lay in the dust with their snouts lying drowsily on their paws. A little fellow was bellowing at the top of his lungs. When he caught sight of Kolya, he stopped. He seemed very surprised to see someone new in the village.

The cat and raven stayed home, but Zhuk ran after the boys, turning up his stump of a tail and glancing haughtily at the sleeping dogs. Aleksandra Petrovna's house was nearby. There was noticeable activity around it.

Two old women stood talking by the front garden. They stopped and looked with curiosity at the boys as they approached. An old man was sitting on the porch. He stepped aside to let the boys pass and silently acknowledged Vladik's greeting. In the entryway, the buzz of voices could be heard. Inside the cottage, a lively argument was going on, in which many people were obviously participating.

"That's strange!" exclaimed Vladik. "Father doesn't like to let outsiders near his patients."

At that very moment the cottage door opened, and Vasily Georgiyevich Golubkov darted into the entryway. He was flushed and excited. His moustache bristled angrily.

"We'll see about that!" he shouted into the cottage, noisily slamming the door. Catching sight of Kolya, he stared at him for a moment, then said,

"Aha, just in the nick of time, young man. . . ."
Grabbing him by the hand, he quickly dragged him along.

Kolya decided Vasily Georgiyevich was angry with him. But he couldn't understand why. The feldsher puffed and panted with indignation. Unable to hold back his rage, he gave Kolya's arm an energetic tug now and then. They went down the porch steps, left the cottage behind, and went into an empty cow barn, where there hadn't been any cows for a long time and where there now lived only a scraggly, emaciated hen.

"Well, young man," said Vasily Georgiyevich, finally releasing Kolya in order to wipe the sweat from his forehead, "who is this little girl, whom you claim as your cousin?"

Kolya froze with fear and kept silent, looking at the ground.

"This is the situation," Vasily Georgiyevich continued. "In her delirium, your cousin announced that she is the daughter of the famous General Rogachov. I would like to know whether or not it's true."

Kolya kept silent, then raised his eyes and said, "She's lying."

"Very well. You mean she's only saying that because she's delirious?"

"She's lying," Kolya repeated stubbornly.

Vasily Georgiyevich gave Kolya a careful, experienced stare. "All right. Now listen, because it
is important for me to find out everything completely and exactly. Your cousin, or whoever she is—
in other words, that girl—talked so much about her
famous father that rumors have traveled throughout
the whole village. Our people would never betray
her. You can depend on it. But there is a certain
man, our village elder, the *starosta*. To be quite
frank, this *starosta* is a swine of swines. It's an ill
wind that blew him into the cottage just as the girl
was babbling on about her father. Our elder decided to go to the *selo* right away to inform the
authorities. Aleksandra Petrovna raised a fuss and
called the people. They immediately gathered in
the cottage where they are now holding him so that
he can't go. But he's dying to get to the *selo* to
report to the commandant's office. Do you see what
I'm driving at?"

"She's dreamed it up," said Kolya. "She heard the
song about Rogachov and made it all up."

Vasily Georgiyevich looked closely at Kolya. "All

right. Then the information isn't dangerous, so I can order them to let the elder go." He turned and made his way resolutely toward the cottage.

"Stop!" Kolya shouted.

Vasily Georgiyevich turned. "Well?"

"You mustn't let the elder go."

"Why not? Is she really Rogachov's daughter?"

"No . . . but. . . ."

Vasily Georgiyevich went over to Kolya and spoke seriously to him. "Kolya, we are all risking our lives by delaying the *starosta*. If she is really Rogachov's daughter, well, what of it? We aren't afraid. But if not, she isn't in any danger, and we are risking our lives needlessly. Look at me and tell the truth."

Kolya raised his eyes. The feldsher stood there, flushed and excited, his moustache bristling and his face so honest that Kolya suddenly made up his mind. "She's telling the truth. General Rogachov is her father."

Vasily Georgiyevich became very businesslike. "So," he said. "How did you find out?"

Kolya told about his grandfather, Ivan Ignatye-vich Solomin, and about the man who came to their forest hideaway; in short, he told everything he knew. The feldsher heard him out, then took him by the hand and silently led him along.

17

Distant Shooting

By the time they entered the cottage, the argument had quieted down a little.

Tossing and turning, Lena was lying on a high bed in a corner. Her eyes were open, but she didn't see anyone. Aleksandra Petrovna was sitting on a chair beside her knitting a sock. About ten peasants, mostly old people, were seated on the floor and on benches along the wall.

A short, thin man with a scraggly, red beard and faded blue eyes was sitting on a chair in the corner. The feldsher went over to Lena, felt her pulse, and touched her forehead.

"Apply cupping glasses again this evening," he said to Aleksandra Petrovna.

"Vasily Georgiyevich," the red-headed man complained, "I must go to the *selo*, or else things aren't likely to turn out well. I'll harness up the horse and be off in a flash. Then everything will be as it should be, and we won't be responsible."

The feldsher turned to a gray-bearded old man, who was bald as a billiard ball. "Did you hear shooting today, Ivan Matveyevich?"

"Yes," the old man answered. "It began this morning."

"Do you think it's artillery?"

"It is," the old man stated with confidence.

"That means they're nearby."

"My little boy told me there's a line of howitzers and tanks on the highway!" a sharp-nosed woman suddenly blurted out. "Officers are sitting in jeeps like kings in a checker game and riding straight to Berlin, if you please."

The man with the red beard put his hand to his cheek in a feminine gesture and started to groan as though he had a toothache. "Oh, oh, oh," he groaned. "What will come of it? Who can I believe? Who should I listen to? If I don't inform, it will go bad for me. But if I do inform, it might go even worse for me." Suddenly he jumped up and bolted for the exit.

By the time he reached the door, a little old man was already seated in front of it so that he couldn't leave. "Wait awhile, Afonkin." the little old man advised in a sweet voice. "The Red Army might come tonight. Then you wouldn't be able to return."

"Oh, oh, oh," Afonkin began to whine again. "My brothers! If you were real people, we could come to an agreement. I could inform right now, and nothing would happen to us. Then, when the Red Army comes, you could protect me, and nothing would happen to me. What do you say, my brothers? What about it, huh?" He looked ingratiatingly at the men seated around, then waved his hand hopelessly. "Inform on me then, confound it" he said in a tearful voice.

The men grinned and looked aside.

"But who can say"—the bald old man shrugged—"whether or not we'll actually have to. . . ."

"Very well," the red-bearded Afonkin said resolutely, "hold me and don't let me go. In three days I must deliver some lists to the *selo*. If I don't take them, they'll come after me. Then we'll see who they arrest."

"But, you see, who can say what will happen?" The bald man grinned again. "In three days' time, you could drown in the river or just up and die."

"Wha-at?" shouted Red Beard. "You want to kill me? Are you threatening me?" He trembled all over. Even his beard was shaking. "When they come from the commandant's office, they'll show you!"

Suddenly an enormous man with a big, gray

beard stood up. He had been quiet until then. He walked silently over to the window and flung it open with a blow of his fist. Everyone looked at him and waited to hear what he had to say. He only raised his finger.

In the silence the distant rumble of firing artillery was distinctly audible.

The old man looked at Red Beard and asked, "Do you hear, Afonkin?" Then he walked over to his place in the corner and sat down just as silently.

Red Beard's groans and sobs began again. "Oh, oh, oh, what should I do? If I inform, it will go bad for me. And if I don't inform, it will go bad for me. How should I act? What should I do?"

Covering his face with the palms of his hands, he rocked back and forth in despair.

"Pah!" exclaimed Vasily Georgiyevich. "Honestly! What trash he is! Take him out, brothers. There's a sick girl here. She needs fresh, clean air."

The villagers took Afonkin home. They kept him confined to the village so that he couldn't tell the Nazis about Lena.

18

Lena's Illness

Day after day went by, but Lena didn't get any better. One minute she was thrashing about in bed, screaming and calling for Kolya, her father, and Grandfather, and complaining that she simply couldn't walk one step farther. The next minute she was calm and quiet, lying there so weak and helpless that even Aleksandra Petrovna, who had seen many a seriously ill person in her day, listened apprehensively to her breathing.

Vasily Georgiyevich Golubkov sat for hours at her bedside. He felt her pulse, tested her hot forehead with his hand, frowned, twitched his moustache, and swore to himself over and over again in a scarcely audible voice.

Kolya and Vladik weren't allowed near Lena. Kolya walked around the cottage for hours on end or stood watch under a tree, trying to catch Lena's every sigh and the feldsher's every word. When they chased him away, he tried to peek in the window; or, gloomy as a cloud, he would sit on the little porch. Vladik didn't succeed even once in persuading him to go for a swim in the lake or just for a short walk in the forest.

"I don't care to," Kolya would answer, turning away. He didn't even want to look at the other boy.

Vladik enlisted the help of Zhuk and the raven. The bird screamed, "Raven! Little raven!" It didn't know how to say anything else. The fox terrier helped by gingerly jerking up his ear and barking upon command. Kolya either sat there gloomily or smiled such an unhappy smile that even Zhuk was put out of countenance and went away, understanding that his performance hadn't been a success.

Sometimes, at the very height of the fox terrier's and raven's antics, Kolya would suddenly ask, "Has your father ever cured pneumonia before?"

"A thousand times," Vladik would assure him. "Maybe even more."

"And are there some . . . well, some that can't be cured?"

"Not Father's patients. That is, of course, there are some cases, but they are very rare."

Kolya would turn away, but even the appearance of his back showed how bad he felt.

"Now don't you worry," his friend constantly

comforted him. "Ask the raven if you want! In the old days, they believed ravens could predict the future."

Kolya looked at the raven doubtfully but asked all the same, "Raven, raven, tell me whether or not Lena will get better."

The raven squinted its eyes slyly and spoke its invariable, "Raven! Little raven!"

"That means she'll get better!" Vladik would declare joyfully.

Still, Kolya always turned away in annoyance. "It doesn't mean anything. Your raven's an idiot. It babbles the same thing all the time."

One night Aleksandra Petrovna knocked on the feldsher's window. Kolya, who couldn't sleep soundly of late and only dozed lightly, immediately jumped out of bed.

Golubkov, pulling on his boots, looked at him angrily and said, "Go back to sleep!"

Kolya knew that arguing with the feldsher would be useless. He sighed deeply, lay back down, and simply gave Golubkov a pleading, mournful look. Vasily Georgiyevich got dressed hurriedly and went out. As soon as the door was closed, Kolya sprang up and began to get dressed.

"Where are you going?" his friend asked sleepily.

Vladik loved to sleep and always slept very soundly.

"Never mind," Kolya answered. "Go to sleep. I'll be right back."

He couldn't bring himself to go into Aleksandra Petrovna's home. He knew the feldsher would be certain to chase him away. Not a single sound was coming from behind the door, and the curtains were drawn. Kolya sat on the little porch, suffering with anguish and fear. He recalled the expression on Vasily Georgiyevich's face. He thought of phrases spoken by Aleksandra Petrovna, compared dozens of little observations, and came to the firm conclusion that the situation was desperate and that Lena was dying, if she hadn't already died.

The moon shone above the village, and long shadows extended from the houses, from the trees, and from the well sweeps. The world was peaceful and majestic in the light of the moon, but a little figure sat cowering on the porch, trembling, sobbing, and terrified.

Vladik came forward quietly and sat down silently beside Kolya. How he loved to sleep, but this time he hadn't slept. The boys sat without speaking for a long time.

Then Kolya turned to Vladik. "Is this a very difficult case?"

"Fiddlesticks! Father has had cases a hundred times more difficult. Even a thousand times more difficult."

The boys stopped talking again. Somewhere in the distance a dog was barking. The moon began to wane noticeably.

"Vladik," asked Kolya, "why was Vasily Georgiyevich so gloomy?"

"Don't be frightened," his friend replied. "He's always that way."

The night dragged on and on. The moon dipped to the edge of the treetops, and stars faded in the east. Roosters began crowing, checking that everything was in order. After reassuring one another, they became quiet again.

Finally the cottage door banged loudly. Kolya and Vladik sprang up.

Golubkov, tired but excited, was standing on the little porch. Catching sight of the boys, he frowned. "Are you here?" he asked in a severe tone of voice. "I thought I told you to sleep."

Kolya didn't answer. He was so worried and upset that he couldn't even breathe.

The feldsher burst out laughing, patted him on the head, and said, "You needn't worry. Lena will get better. The crisis has passed, and her temperature has fallen."

19

A Short Rest

As soon as Lena began to recover, Kolya took a great liking to village life. The old people, who were the only adult inhabitants left in the village, treated him very well. Kolya grew to be as friendly with Vasily Georgiyevich and Aleksandra Petrovna as if he had grown up with them.

The feldsher was witty, energetic, and quick-tempered. When his face got red and his moustache bristled, Kolya and Vladik kept quiet and tried to get away unnoticed. But Golubkov calmed down with surprising speed. He would bang his fist on the table, look down at it, then burst out laughing.

He had spent thirty years in this part of the country. Fourteen years ago, he had married. Shortly afterward his wife had died, leaving him a son. Vasily Georgiyevich brought Vladik up by himself. While the boy was small, he fed him with a spoon, gave him his bath, and even mended his trousers.

Aleksandra Petrovna had tried to take over these responsibilities herself, but the feldsher had told her sharply that he would manage on his own.

When Vladik was ten years old, his father began to initiate him into his work and talk things over with him as he would with a grown-up. The boy knew the symptoms of many illnesses. Whenever father and son discussed serious questions such as how to make do without money, for example, or whether they should accept a chicken that Granny Alekseyeva had brought them out of gratitude for being cured, they appeared to be two men, two fellow workers, talking.

Kolya and Vladik became very good friends. Kolya hadn't had a friend his own age for a long time. After all Lena was considerably younger, and he was used to taking a protective attitude toward her. He and Vladik often went to a little lake a short distance from the village, where they could have running and swimming races. Zhuk went with them. The cat liked to stay home and lie on the stove. The raven, which was two hundred years old according to Vladik, would accompany them for a very short way, then hastily return home. The raven was afraid of new places.

Before long Lena began to get better. There were always people at her bedside. The old people brought presents and asked about her father and her life. They gave Ivan Ignatyevich Solomin high praise, saying he was obviously a good and clever man. They approved of Kolya. Others his age teased dogs, they claimed, but he had saved Lena and not fallen into the hands of the Nazis.

Every morning the boys visited Lena, sometimes bringing the raven, who would amuse her by screaming, "Raven! Little raven!" The fox terrier would walk on his hind legs or play dead as Lena laughed and clapped her hands. Afterward the boys went to the lake. Golubkov released Vladik from his work and didn't give him any errands to do while Kolya was there. Later in the day they visited Lena again, and everyone ate dinner at Aleksandra Petrovna's. They ran around the village after dinner, sometimes visiting a neighbor or chatting with Vasily Georgiyevich.

The village was off the beaten track, far away from towns and *selos*. Rarely did a stranger ever come by. The German occupation affected it very little. The Nazis knew that such remote places weren't garrisoned, and they didn't visit often, since they were rather afraid of traveling forest roads. The only representative of Hitler's power in the village was Afonkin, the *starosta*. He drew up lists for the dispatch of people to Germany. He had betrayed and handed over to the Germans Widow Morgunova's daughter, who had been hiding in a cellar. The peasants would have settled accounts with him long ago, except that the Germans burned down villages and shot the inhabitants for murdering their village elders.

Now that artillery fire could be distinctly heard, and the front was apparently getting closer every day, the *starosta* began to have bad dreams at night. The peasants bided their time and didn't even their score with him, waiting for the Soviet units to arrive. But the village elder was afraid of the peasants and decided not to contradict them. They didn't allow him out of the village and dogged his very footsteps.

After three days, when the time came for the *starosta* to take his lists to the *selo*, they made him write a letter saying he was sick and was sending a proxy in his place. Afonkin was beside himself, but could do nothing. They chose as proxy an old man who was stone-deaf and who solemnly promised not

to catch a single question asked him. The old man
went off and returned safely the next day toward
evening.

Despite the fact that he was deaf and weak
sighted, he knew perfectly well how to hear and
see what was necessary. He told the villagers that
a continuous line of transport units and columns of
jeeps were headed westward down the highway,
that the Nazis were very sullen and moody, and that
some important Hitlerite had already run out of
town; in a word, things seemed to be drawing to
an end.

Afonkin became very worried and uneasy. He
asked everyone to remember that he hadn't wanted
to serve as *starosta* and that he had tried to save
whomever he could. All was a lie. When the villagers told him so, he grew melancholy and depressed. Nevertheless, they decided to keep him
under guard so that he could not leave the village.

That evening everyone gathered on the street to
listen to the firing. It could be heard very clearly.
At first they thought it was being carried on a fair
wind, but there turned out to be no wind at all.
The front was simply coming closer with the passing of each twenty-four hours. Kolya ran to tell

Lena, and she got excited. Lately she thought constantly about meeting her father. She asked everyone if they thought he would recognize her. After all she certainly had changed in the past three years. What if he didn't recognize his own daughter?

The next day Lena went out on the street for the first time. Kolya and Vladik had visited her earlier that morning. All the housewives spoke to her and invited her in. Zhuk jumped around, wagging his stub of a tail. The raven screamed, "Raven! Little raven!" endlessly. And the cat that didn't like to leave the house went out onto the little porch in honor of the occasion.

For the following day they planned to fix a festive dinner in celebration of Lena's recovery. First of all, there had to be fish soup, made from fish that Vladik had caught. Secondly, there must be mushrooms. Last of all, there had to be berries, which Kolya would pick.

That evening Vasily Georgiyevich Golubkov was called urgently to a village twenty kilometers away, where there was a sick woman who needed immediate help. The feldsher put his instruments into his doctor's bag and set out after promising to return soon. He didn't return until the next day toward evening. He was depressed and gloomy. At the dinner table he kept silent, sniffing with displeasure and bristling his moustache. After eating, Lena went to bed. She was still weak from her illness, so she had to go to bed early. Vasily Georgiyevich then blurted out, "It turns out they're searching for Lena in the neighboring village."

Kolya shuddered with the unexpectedness of this remark. He opened his eyes wide.

"Yes, yes. It's true," the feldsher continued. "They have already been to the village I visited. They interrogated the inhabitants about whether or not a little boy and girl had passed through. They'll probably be here soon."

During the days spent at the feldsher's, Kolya had settled down and stopped feeling like a defenseless, pursued runaway. All danger had seemed to be past. He thought they had only to wait peacefully for the arrival of Soviet troops. Then he would take Lena to Rogachov, and everything would be all right.

He was seized with despair at the thought that they must run and hide again to save themselves. The expression on his face was probably very sad, because Golubkov smiled and patted him on the head.

"Never mind, Kolya," he said. "Don't lose heart! Maybe there's still a chance they won't come here. If they do, then we'll hide. And if we can't hide, we'll run away together."

20

A Fishing Trip

Next morning Vladik dug some worms, took a fishing pole, and set out for the lake. Kolya, who intended to pick berries, took along a big basket. Lena wanted to go with him, but Golubkov wouldn't let her.

"It's out of the question," he said. "Rest and get a lot to eat. You might need your strength soon."

Kolya picked a full basket of berries in short order. Wild strawberries were excellent in these parts, and raspberries were beginning to ripen, too. When there was no room for any more berries, Kolya decided to visit Vladik at the lake. His friend was sitting on a rock in the shadow of a big willow, attentively watching his float. It was hot even here near the lake. Bumblebees buzzed monotonously. A transparent, pale-blue dragonfly flitted by, and water bugs skidded across the water.

"How's it going?" Kolya asked.

Vladik nodded silently toward the bucket, in

which ten small fish were splashing. Kolya sat down on a rotten tree trunk that had been blown over in a long-ago storm. It was too hot to talk. Vladik pulled up his fishing pole, but the fish got away. He threw his line out again. The float lay on the water, swaying smoothly in the lake's gentle ripples.

"When the Nazis are driven out, will you and Lena go to town to live?" asked Vladik.

"Yes, of course," Kolya answered. He was surprised that Vladik asked. His friend sat without moving, looking closely at the float.

"Grandfather said we'll be given another place to live if our house is destroyed," Kolya continued.

He stopped talking. The dragonfly settled down beside him on the tree trunk. He watched its blue wings flutter. A gadfly buzzed near Kolya's ear, but he felt too lazy to shoo it away.

"Father and I will stay here," Vladik declared suddenly. "Father has become accustomed to our village."

He spoke quietly, even indifferently, but Kolya sensed that he was very sad about staying. "Fiddlesticks!" Kolya exclaimed confidently. "You'll have to go to school."

"Well, what of it? There's a school here."

"Where? In the *selo*? Ten kilometers away?"

"Why not? There used to be a boarding school there. After the war there will be one again." Vladik yanked his fishing pole. A perch flashed through the air and fell onto the grass.

"A big one!" exclaimed Kolya.

"Yes, not bad."

Vladik dropped the perch into the bucket, put another worm on the hook, and threw the line out again.

"Fiddlesticks!" Kolya repeated. "Since you're going to have to go to boarding school anyway, it would be better to spend the winter in town and go to the ten-year school there. Before you know it, you'll be in the eighth class. You can live with us. You and I will share a room, and Grandfather will have the other room."

He felt sad himself when he happened to think that Lena wouldn't be with them. Somehow the thought had never entered his head that Lena and he would have to part after he took her to her father. Of course, they would probably still see each other now and then, but things wouldn't be the same. They wouldn't study and play together or listen to Grandfather's stories every night.

"If your grandfather agrees to it, maybe Father will let me go."

"He'll agree," Kolya said confidently. "Why wouldn't he?"

"Will Lena go to Moscow?" Vladik asked.

"Yes," Kolya answered, deep in thought. "She'll probably go to Moscow."

Again a silvery perch flashed through the air and fell onto the grass. Kolya watched silently as Vladik baited the hook and threw out the line.

The float swayed in the water again, and once more the boys were silent. The dragonfly left, flying over the grass, its wings sparkling and fluttering.

Now Vladik sensed that Kolya was sad. "Has your grandfather been teaching you these last few years?" he asked.

"Yes. If Zapolsk is freed by the beginning of the school year, I'll be going into the sixth class."

"Me, too. That means we'll finish ten-year school in five years. Then we'll enter the University at Moscow."

Vladik spoke so quietly in such a businesslike way that Kolya was convinced. For the first time in his life, he pictured himself with certainty as a university student.

"What will you study to be?" he asked.

"A doctor," Vladik answered. "How about you?"

"I don't know what it's called. . . . A zoologist, I think. Is there a zoological institute?"

"There must be one in Moscow."

"Well, I will study there then."

Vladik yanked his fishing pole, and a small fish flopped onto the grass. He put it in the bucket, baited the hook, and threw the line out again. "We'll be together," he said. "We'll ask to be roommates."

"On Sundays, we'll buy tickets to the theater," Kolya continued, "and visit Lena. Have you ever ridden a streetcar?"

"No, but I know how."

"Me, too. We'll take walks in the park in summer. . . ."

The boys stopped talking.

"A doctor and a zoologist," mused Vladik. "Those are similar professions."

"Quite similar," Kolya repeated, taking up Vladik's line of thought. "They have many required subjects in common. We'll probably have to study a lot of the same courses."

"We'll go to classes together. . . ." Vladik suddenly broke off and became silent.

"In summer," said Kolya, "we'll go off to Zapolsk with Lena. We'll grow moustaches for the fun of it, and Grandfather won't recognize us. We'll say, 'How do you do? We bring greetings from Moscow.'"

The float jerked, went underwater, then bobbed to the surface again.

"A bite! It must be a big one."

"Sh-h!" warned Vladik. "Be quiet, or he'll notice. . . ."

Kolya's friend was looking beyond the lake, where a path wound along the slope of a forest-covered hill. A man was walking down the path. He kept disappearing momentarily behind some trees, then appearing again.

At first Kolya didn't even understand why Vladik was afraid. So, a man was out walking! Well, let him go!

But this time the man came out from behind a tree trunk slowly and carefully, as if he were ready to hide again at the slightest warning. He looked around the forest. The boys sat without moving. They couldn't be seen among the alternating green leaves and white birch trunks.

The man went a little farther. He seemed excited and disturbed, and he kept looking around, walking stealthily, like a thief. Before he disappeared over the top of the hill, Kolya recognized him. He was Afonkin, the *starosta*.

"Vladik!" Kolya exclaimed, perplexed. "What does this mean? Did they let him go?"

Vladik hastily got together his fishing gear. "Let's go," he said. "There's no time to lose."

21

An Important Decision

The boys took quick strides, talking as little as possible so that they wouldn't get out of breath. Near the cottage, Zhuk greeted them with joyful barking.

Lena poked her head out the window and shouted, "Did you catch many fish? Wow! What a lot of berries!"

Without answering, the boys climbed the porch steps and went into the house. Vasily Georgiyevich was seated at the table sorting out old notes. Glancing at the boys, he knew right away that something had happened.

"Well, what's the matter?" he asked, frowning.

Vladik answered his question with another question. "Papa, where's Afonkin?"

"Afonkin?" The feldsher's frown deepened. "Aleksandr Timofeyevich is guarding him."

"No, he isn't. Afonkin has escaped. We saw him.

He was walking down the path over the big hill, going toward the *selo*."

"Nonsense! That's impossible."

Lena didn't understand what the conversation was all about, but she guessed by their tone of voice that something bad had happened. Her face immediately fell, and her eyes got round as saucers. Vasily Georgiyevich looked at her and got up.

"Let's go find out," he said.

Aleksandr Timofeyevich, a little old man with a goatee, was sitting on the porch of the *starosta*'s cottage. He was taking pleasure in smoking unhurriedly and enjoying the sun, its warmth, and the peaceful quiet.

"Is Afonkin home?" asked Vasily Georgiyevich.

"He's sleeping." Aleksandr Timofeyevich grinned. "There's nothing for him to do, so for days now he's been spending his time sleeping. It's not life. It's a sanatorium." He sniffed and coughed.

Golubkov silently climbed the porch steps and went into the cottage. The boys and the guard followed him. They saw at once that the *starosta* wasn't there. The cottage was empty, and a little window overlooking the garden was wide open.

Vasily Georgiyevich grunted and sat down on a

stool. "He was yawning! He fell asleep! Death would be too good for you!" he screamed at the guard. Without listening to the excuses of the embarrassed old man, he walked out of the cottage.

Within ten minutes a "military council" took place in the home of Aleksandra Petrovna. Golubkov paced from one corner of the room to the other with heavy steps. Aleksandra Petrovna was sitting on a stool at the table, sewing a jacket for Kolya. Vladik, Kolya, and Lena were seated on the bed, listening silently.

"We can't stay here," said Vasily Georgiyevich. "A little girl isn't a needle. We can't hide her in a cellar. This is a small village. It wouldn't take long to search it. We'll gather some things and go into the forest. Who would find us there? We'll live like Indians for a week, and afterward we'll even have a good time remembering it."

Aleksandra Petrovna bit off her thread and smoothed out on the table the piece she had been sewing. "A good time!" she said. "In the first place, they could find you. Maybe accidentally. Or the *starosta* could put them on the track. Or they could simply comb the forest. Secondly, when Hitler's men set foot in this territory, all kinds of riffraff will be wandering around the woods. No, it won't work."

Golubkov snorted, looking at Aleksandra Petrovna angrily, but he didn't contradict her. He began pacing the room again.

"That means we must go to another village," he said. "One where they've already looked for Lena. We'll hide there and probably be back in less than a week."

"You can't hide in a village," Aleksandra Petrovna quietly objected. "If a man like Afonkin lives in our own village, then imagine what kind of scoundrel you might come across in another village."

Vasily Georgiyevich snorted even louder and stomped across the floor even harder. "Well, then, what do you propose?"

"That you go to Zapolsk. Which of your old friends is still there? Is Konushkin there?"

"I believe so."

"Well, there you are. Konushkin will hide you. And if not Konushkin, then somebody else. It would never enter anyone's head to search for you in town."

Again Vasily Georgiyevich snorted but didn't find any objection. "We must leave right away," he said in such a tone that one would think there never had been any question at all about where they were going.

They didn't leave right away. By the time they got together some food for the road and said their good-bys to Aleksandra Petrovna and Vladik, whom his father refused to take despite his pleas, two hours had passed.

The sun had already dipped toward the west when the feldsher, Kolya, and Lena were skirting the lake. The village was hidden behind the forest.

"You know what?" said Vasily Georgiyevich. "Let's not follow the path. We might meet someone there! Let's go straight through the forest."

They passed under the cool shade of a birch. After going around the tree and picking their way through some bushes, they reached the top of a hill. From there the village and the lake, which looked like a plate lying on green grass, became visible again. A path twisted downward. The tops of enormous trees were swaying; the wind was cool and refreshing. Looking at familiar places from such a height was pleasant.

Suddenly the feldsher grabbed the children by the hand and pulled them behind a tree. Headed in the direction of the village, a man was walking hurriedly up the path. Kolya stuck his head out from behind the tree trunk and recoiled. He immediately recognized the coarse linen trousers, the shirt, the knapsack hanging from one shoulder, and the sleeve tucked into the belt.

"It's him!" Kolya whispered. "It's him, Vasily Georgiyevich! The one-armed man!"

The feldsher groaned and carefully looked out from behind the tree trunk. The one-armed man appeared to be in a big hurry. He was walking without glancing around, hastening his step more and more. He disappeared behind the trees, appeared again, then finally was gone around the bend.

"Yes," exclaimed Vasily Georgiyevich, "we left the village in the nick of time! If we had delayed another hour, we would have been cooked like a chicken dropped into cabbage soup."

From then on they walked without stopping until the sun set. Golubkov carried Lena on his shoulders during the last hour, so they walked along much more slowly. All in all the feldsher was dissatisfied.

"We haven't gone very far at all!" he said. "At this rate, it will take us more than three days to get to town."

But nothing could be done. Lena tired easily after her illness. Going faster was out of the question. They spent the night under a big pine tree and fell asleep right away. The sun had already risen by the time they awoke. The feldsher, after some hesitation, decided to make a little fire and prepare some tea.

Once breakfast was finished, they were on their way. It wasn't very far to a country road.

22

The Center of a Whirlpool

They expected to reach the country road by noon. At eleven o'clock they heard voices. Kolya crept up to find out what was going on, and upon returning reported that a German battery was by the roadside and artillerymen were prowling around the area. They decided to keep walking straight through the forest.

They went along safely for three kilometers. Suddenly a shot rang out. The bullet, flying over Lena's head, hit a young birch. The feldsher pushed the children down onto the grass and fell beside them. He was just in time, for a second bullet immediately whistled by.

This time Kolya noticed where the shooting was coming from. A man was standing behind a big, tall pine. He leaned out from behind the tree, took a shot, and hid again.

Their position was futile and dangerous. They didn't know who the man was or what he wanted.

Golubkov took out an enormous Mauser and looked it over with considerable misgiving. Apparently he didn't have a clear idea of how to shoot it. The stranger ran behind a tree nearer them. He was wearing a German uniform without the cap and holding a pistol in his hand. Vasily Georgiyevich jerked up the Mauser and squeezed the trigger firmly. The Mauser was as silent as if it had a curse on it. The feldsher, cussing and swearing, began to tinker with it. Deciding that his enemy didn't have a weapon, the stranger grew bolder.

"Give up! Give yourselves up!" he shouted in Russian, quickly crawling forward.

He was already very close. Golubkov kept fussing with the gun, cursing the "idiotic contraption" all the while. The Mauser went off unexpectedly. Although the bullet just missed Kolya's ear and went somewhere far into the forest, the stranger fell to his knees and raised his hands. The feldsher jumped up. Waving his Mauser as though he might be induced to shoot it at any minute, he ran forward.

The stranger was kneeling with raised hands. "I'm a deserter! A German deserter!" he said.

Vasily Georgiyevich frowned. "All right," he said, "but just the same, you stay there, and we'll stay here." He indicated opposite directions.

The deserter smiled joyfully and repeated, "You —there, we—here."

Kolya bent down and picked up the pistol the man had thrown aside.

They walked on, looking back all the while and pointing both the Mauser and pistol at the German. After proceeding about one hundred steps, they stopped being on their guard and turned their backs on the stranger. A shot rang out. Evidently the man had another pistol. Golubkov's face got red. Bellowing with rage, he rushed after the deserter. Their enemy, seeing that he had missed, waved his hands and hid behind a tree.

"What in blue blazes!" exclaimed Vasily Georgiyevich. "You have to have eyes in the back of your head. Now they're beginning to wander about the forest."

But the forest seemed deserted. After selecting a spot closed in on all sides by bushes, they ate. Then they walked on. They came to the highway toward dusk. When they saw it, they knew right away that they could not get across it. An uninterrupted stream of German troop convoys were going down the road. Drivers were urging on peasants' horses, which were loaded down with military belongings and officers' trunks. On wagons came war machinery, officers and their women, traveling cases, baskets and boxes. Heavy guns lumbered along noisily. With a deafening roar, motorcycles tried to jump among the jeeps. Horns honked, motors rumbled, drivers cursed, horses neighed, and officers shouted, brandishing pistols.

"Yes, indeed," said the feldsher, "this is an interesting sight! Still, we're going to have to swim across this raging river."

They stood, hidden by the bushes, and watched the impassable stream. Dusk thickened. It was almost dark, but vehicles kept rolling by and the troop convoys dragged on. Big guns rumbled past. There was no end to the procession.

When it was completely dark, Soviet airplanes, which appeared from behind the forest, began flying overhead. They threw down flares that hung over the road with their bright lights and slowly descended, illuminating everything around. They were patrol planes. Although they didn't shoot at the road or drop bombs, they created a terrible panic.

Snorting horses pulled wagons across stumps, windfallen branches, and roots. Vehicles sideswiped tree trunks, and pine branches tore tarpaulins from wagons and trucks.

The feldsher and the children found themselves in the center of a whirlpool. They could be clearly seen through the thin bushes, but in the general panic nobody paid any attention to them.

The airplanes flew away. Flares died out in the sky. The vehicles, jeeps, and pedestrians began to return to the road. At that very moment, Vasily Georgiyevich grabbed Lena and Kolya by the hand. They quickly ran across the road. Now, too, no one paid any attention to them. Behind them, horns started blowing again, horses neighed, and motorcycles began roaring. The noise gradually died down.

Soon the forest was silent and deserted. At last the trees parted. In the starry, obscure light lay the abandoned town of Zapolsk, where life had come to a standstill.

23

Underground

The fugitives slunk along the empty, silent streets. There didn't seem to be a single person in the whole town. The feldsher stopped in front of a little one-story house with tightly locked shutters. He knocked. No one answered. He knocked louder. Still louder. He started beating on the door with all his might.

Finally somewhere below, as if underground, a man's voice warned, "Watch out! We have weapons. We'll shoot." Evidently turning to someone else, he added, "Vaska, get the machine gun!"

"Why you fool!" the feldsher retorted angrily. "I must see Konushkin. Konushkin, the agriculturist. Do you understand?"

"And who are you?" the voice below asked.

"I'm his friend, Vasily Georgiyevich Golubkov. Pass my name on to him, if he's there."

Only then did Kolya realize the voice was coming from the cellar window.

"My God," the voice answered, "Vasily Georgi-yevich! Is it you, dear friend?"

"Who's that?" the feldsher asked nervously.

"It's me, Yevstigneyev!"

"Oh, you old simpleton," Golubkov bellowed. "Why are you hiding underground? Come out here, and I'll kiss you!"

"No, it would be better for you to come in here," said Yevstigneyev. "Nowadays it's safer in a cellar."

"Listen, Petya. In the first place, where did you get a machine gun? In the second place, where is Konushkin? I must see him, you understand."

"As for the machine gun, I was just bluffing. And Konushkin is at his new apartment. Officers were living here, so he had to move to a new place. Do you know where Yelizaveta Karpovna used to live? He's there. Probably in the cellar like us."

"Then so long, Petya," Vasily Georgiyevich said. "I'm going to see him."

"All right," said Yevstigneyev. "Maybe tomorrow our men will come. We'll see one another then. Someone was here earlier today asking for Konush-kin. 'Isn't Konushkin here?' he asked. 'No, he isn't,' I said. 'What about Golubkov? Vasily Georgiyevich? Is he by any chance here?' 'Why, I remember him!' I answered. 'But I haven't seen him for two years.'"

"Someone asked about me?" quizzed the feldsher, becoming upset. "Who?"

"How would I know?" the underground voice answered. "What could I see from here? Only two feet. And I couldn't see them very well."

Vasily Georgiyevich tugged at Lena's and Kolya's hands. "All right, let's go."

Once again they walked down the dark, empty street. The distant exchange of gunfire could be heard. The *rat-a-tat-tat* of a machine gun came from somewhere. A desperate cry rang out, and everything quieted down. Suddenly artillery opened fire. It struck with such deafening strength that they could hear glass rattling in the houses. The dark sky was lighted with flashes, and the roar of explosions merged into one incessant boom.

"Quick, quick!" Vasily Georgiyevich hurried the children. "We seem to have fallen straight into a pot of hot kasha."

They ran up to the house where Konushkin was supposed to be. Now and then, when the sky glowed with fire, streets sprang out of the darkness, then disappeared again. Houses, front gardens, and trees growing along sidewalks appeared momentarily. The town seemed deserted.

The front was already so close that the police, the

Bürgermeister, and the entire staff of the commandant's office had hurriedly fled. Inhabitants who had survived the three-year occupation were hiding in cellars. Only once did they see someone running across the street, a madman dressed in a sack with holes cut out for his head and arms.

"Drive the balls with your feet!" he was shouting. "Drive the little balls with your feet!" Despair and terror were in his voice. He dashed by. Once more they heard from afar, "The little balls! Drive the balls with your feet!"

The streets became lifeless again. Artillery boomed louder and louder in the distance. Somewhere, seemingly nearby, tanks started to rumble. The din increased until it permeated everything, then died down. The tanks passed by.

The two-story house in which Konushkin was staying seemed high in this town of one-story houses. Vasily Georgiyevich banged on the door with all his might.

Again they heard a voice below them, as if underground. "Who's there? What do you want?"

"Konushkin," said Vasily Georgiyevich, "it's me, Golubkov. Feldsher Golubkov."

"At last!" the underground voice said. "Go to the right. You'll see an entrance into the cellar."

They ran along the house, went down a short flight of stairs, and found the door already open. They entered a dark, damp corridor and walked down it quickly. In front of them was a big, low apartment. People were coming to meet them. Yelping with joy, a fox terrier, the very one that belonged to Vladik, jumped at Kolya and rubbed against his legs. Vladik himself was standing there. He smiled and gave Kolya his hand.

Suddenly Kolya heard a voice he remembered very well. "At last! I was beginning to think I'd never meet up with you."

He turned. Before him stood the one-armed man, smiling triumphantly. The shock was like a nightmare.

Grabbing Lena by the hand, Kolya ran out into the corridor. The last thing he saw was the puzzled expression on the one-armed man's face. Kolya slammed the door and dragged Lena quickly down the corridor. He shut the outside door, too, and slipped the iron bolt into place. Their tormentor was locked in the cellar. They could catch their breath for a second.

"Kolya, why are you running? What happened?"

"It's him—the one-armed man. . . . We must escape. Do you understand, Lena?"

"Why is Vladik there?" the astonished Lena wondered. "Why is Vasily Georgiyevich there?"

"I don't know. I don't know anything. I just know this—I must save you from that man."

The people inside banged on the door. "Kolya," they shouted. "Kolya, open up!"

"Let's run!" Kolya commanded.

They ran down the empty street. At the corner, Kolya stopped and looked back. The light from the cellar window was shining onto the street. One after another, dark figures were climbing out of the cellar. When an outbreak of firing illuminated the street, Kolya caught sight of Zhuk dashing after him.

He jerked Lena's hand and ran down a side street. They gasped for breath, their pulse pounding loudly in their ears. Behind them, they heard the footsteps and shouts of their pursuers.

Perhaps the most terrifying thing of all was Zhuk, the good little dog who had changed from a friend into a relentless enemy. He unfailingly and silently (that was especially frightening) persisted in tracking them down.

Yes, indeed, everything was just like a bad dream.

With the dog close on their heels, they ran down a side street. They heard the clicking of his claws on the sidewalk pavement. Kolya turned. In the semidarkness, the dog seemed to be smiling. Kolya screamed and kicked him with all his might. The fox terrier rolled aside. By this time their pursuers were already running toward them from the street corner.

Kolya and Lena made another turn. The side street went up a hill. Running uphill was very difficult. Lena was gasping for breath. Kolya had to tug at her hand harder and harder. The street curved, turning abruptly into a wall. Kolya understood in a flash. They were in a blind alley. This trap also was like a nightmare. There was no way out. It was too late to run back. They could hear the hastening footsteps of their tormentors. Kolya looked around in despair.

"Maybe we shouldn't run anymore. Let them catch us and do what they want with us. I can't go on, Kolya!"

In the darkness, the boy heard Lena sobbing. His whole body shook with terror and pity. "Little Lena," he said, gasping for breath, "of course, we should keep running. Just a little longer. Just till tomorrow. Our own soldiers will be here then. You know what I've thought up? I have a pistol. You run, and I'll shoot it out with them. I'll hold them

off while you hide somewhere in the gateway.
Quick! Quick!"

He pulled the pistol out of his pocket and pushed
her. She didn't move.

"No," she said sadly and quietly, "I won't leave
you, Kolya. What would I do without you?"

These words filled Kolya's heart with such thank-
fulness and tenderness that he gave her a hug and a
big kiss.

Calming down a little, they stepped onto the stoop
of a nearby house. Kolya took out the pistol. Their
pursuers appeared around the bend. A burst of explosions illuminated them. They were standing in
the middle of the road in a group, deliberating.
Zhuk was running around, twirling his stub of a tail.

There was nothing Kolya and Lena could do.
They had to wait.

Kolya saw their black silhouettes clearly during
the outbursts of firing. He didn't attempt to shoot,
but he knew he wouldn't miss when the time came.

The deliberation ended. Vasily Georgiyevich
(Kolya recognized him at once) stepped forward
resolutely. The others stood and waited. "Kolya!"
he shouted. "Kolya, it's me! Don't you recognize
me?"

"Don't come any closer, Vasily Georgiyevich!" Kolya answered. "I recognize you. I don't know why you're helping them catch us, but I won't give up all the same."

"Wait a minute, Kolya," the feldsher said. "Don't be alarmed. Listen to what I have to say first. I have a letter in my hand. Here it is. Can you see it?" He waved a little square of paper. "It's very important that you read it. It's addressed to you. I'll put it into Zhuk's mouth. He'll bring it to you. You'll be able to read it during the outbreaks of firing. Then, if you want, we'll go away, and you and Lena can go wherever you like. Is it a deal, Kolya?"

Kolya considered the proposition quickly. There didn't seem to be any harm in it. On the other hand, all these grown-ups were more clever and experienced than he. He thought over the feldsher's proposal again. Then he thought it through once more. No, nothing seemed to be wrong with it.

"All right," he shouted. "Send the dog!"

Vasily Georgiyevich gave the command, and the fox terrier ran to Kolya with the letter between his teeth. The feldsher went back. All four people in the group stood motionless, without making any attempt to get closer. Kolya grabbed the letter. Zhuk began to wag his stub of a tail. He ran over to Lena and stood on his hind legs. An explosion lighted up the street.

In the letter was written: "Dear Kolya, the man who will give you this letter. . . ."

Darkness fell. There was no doubt of one thing—the handwriting was Ivan Ignatyevich's. There was another outbreak of firing.

"The one-armed man, whom I told you to beware of. . . ."

Darkness again. If only the explosions would come closer together! Light again.

". . . is not an enemy, but a friend. He must take Lena where she is supposed to go, and you. . . ."

Again darkness and a new outbreak of firing.

"Trust him. I repeat. He is a friend and was sent by friends. Your grandfather."

Kolya sat down on the stoop and burst out crying. He cried while the terrible man, of whom he had been so afraid, hugged him with his only arm. He cried when Vladik and the feldsher tapped him on the shoulder. And he cried while someone he didn't know, who turned out to be Konushkin the agriculturist, hurried them along, saying the streets were dangerous and that they should get into the cellar as soon as possible. He was still sobbing when they were seated in the cellar drinking tea and when Zhuk, wagging his stub of a tail, was rushing happily first to him, then to Lena.

24

A Long Night

The one-armed man, whose name was Ivan Tarasovich Gurov, held out a package of sugar to Lena and said, smiling, "It looks as though I have a chance to treat you again. I hope you won't run away this time."

Lena laughed, and so did everyone else. Now that Kolya knew Gurov wasn't an enemy he had to escape, the one-armed man seemed surprisingly kind and pleasant. His facial expression had seemed sly to Kolya before, but now it was merry and good, without having changed a bit in reality.

This impression seemed odd to Kolya. He didn't hold back and told Gurov about it. Everyone laughed again. Gurov laughed loudest.

When the laughter died down, Ivan Tarasovich began telling the children about his search for Lena.

"When Doctor Krechetov was arrested, his sister was taken to the commandant's office. There she let out the secret that Rogachov's daughter was living

somewhere on a lonely farm in the forest with Solomin, the schoolteacher. Whether she hoped to save
her brother or whether she's just a mean, wicked
woman is hard to say. At any rate, the Nazis hung
the doctor and became very interested in Rogachov's daughter. They hunted everywhere but
couldn't find you, since you lived in such a secluded
place. A certain deaf old man worked as a mes-
senger in the Zapolsk commandant's office. They
kept him because of his being deaf, thinking that
he wouldn't hear a thing. They spoke quite openly
in his presence. Actually the old man wasn't deaf
at all. He heard everything he had to hear quite
well and was constantly giving the commander of
our detachment important news. He passed on old
lady Krechetova's story. Until then everyone pre-
sumed that Rogachov's family had died in the bombing. Having found out for certain that Rogachov's
daughter was alive, we decided to search for her."

Gurov took out a cigarette and began smoking. It
was bright, even cozy, there in the cellar. In addition to Lena, Kolya, Vladik, Konushkin, Golubkov,
and Gurov, there was a good-natured old woman,
who poured tea, and her little grandson, who was
sleeping blissfully, as though there were no sign of
war. Artillery kept firing, but they were used to it

and didn't pay any attention. Sometimes they heard the distant rumble of a tank. Then everyone became quiet and listened. The tanks always passed by.

The conversation continued. Gurov went on to say that every intelligence officer was given the job of inquiring about Solomin and finding out where he lived. No news turned up for a long time. Hope had been almost entirely abandoned when a young fellow returned with information, saying, "There is a rumor going around about Solomin. They say he lives with his grandson and granddaughter on a remote farm. The farm is supposedly in this vicinity."

Ivan Tarasovich Gurov told how the commander of the detachment, upon hearing the man's story, had sent for him and ordered him to go to Solomin, reveal his identity, and take the little girl.

"It's difficult for you to fight in battles with only one arm," the commander had told him, "but here is a chance for you to do a good deed. When the plane comes our way again, we'll put this little girl on it. We'll give General Rogachov a priceless gift."

Ivan Tarasovich put out his cigarette, poured himself some tea, and broke off a piece of sugar.

Unexpectedly big guns thundered nearby. They were much closer than before. The old woman gave Ivan Tarasovich a frightened look.

"Never mind, granny," Gurov explained. "Don't worry. That's one of Hitler's batteries. They'll shoot a bit, then go on. The Nazis have no fortifications whatsoever here. I can tell you that for certain. Their fortifications were fifty kilometers away. Now they have to fall back another thirty kilometers. They'll probably try to hold out at the river. Since Zapolsk is off the main road and is by no means a good defensive position, I don't foresee any serious action here. Of course, there will be street skirmishes. Maybe a few tanks will try to linger on, but I don't think anything very terrible can happen."

"Oh, dearie," sighed the old woman, "maybe now we'll know for sure where it's safe and where it isn't!"

"Yes. Now where were we?" Ivan Tarasovich continued. "I set out for Solomin's, and, well, you already know how he fooled me. I came back from the lake and told him he had played a clever trick on me but that he'd live to regret it. I explained who I was and why I was looking for Lena. The old man really did regret deeply what he'd done. He said he didn't know where to look for you children himself but that you must be traveling by steamboat. In his excitement, he didn't warn me that he'd ordered you to beware the one-armed man.

"When the boat left and you didn't return, I understood what was going on. How I scolded myself! I was very much afraid that you'd fall into old lady Krechetova's hands. After all you didn't know she was the one who had given you away. I didn't manage to intercept you on the way. I didn't succeed in getting in touch with my own people either, and I had to conduct myself very carefully in town. Many people there knew me, because I had worked at the printing house for ten years.

"When the roundup of children began, I knew they were looking for you. But I didn't know where you were hiding. I was informed you had managed to escape. Our men began looking for you along all the roads and in all the villages. You had vanished into thin air."

Ivan Tarasovich told how Hitler's men began tackling the problem energetically. Apparently they had decided that come what may they would take Rogachov's daughter with them when they retreated. Gurov had been very worried about the children. The head of his detachment gave him a good dressing down and made him feel ashamed.

He decided to make the rounds of the nearest villages. He was in them all but couldn't find out anything until he set out for the one where Kolya and

Lena were living. On the way he met a sly old man with a red beard. He asked him how to get to the village. The old fellow gave him directions.

"Are you from there?" Gurov asked.

"I am."

"And did a boy and girl come to live in your village a short while ago?"

The old man looked at him intently and asked, "Are you looking for those children?"

"Yes," Ivan Tarasovich answered, "I'm looking for them."

"Are you looking for the girl?"

"Yes, the girl."

Gurov didn't understand anything at that point but decided to find out as cautiously as possible why the old man was questioning him. He played right along with him for the time being.

"Did they instruct you to find her?" Red Beard asked.

"Yes."

"Why?"

"I can't tell you that."

"Whose daughter is she? Do you know?"

"I know," Gurov answered.

"Whose?"

"You say it first."

"No, you."

They argued and argued but couldn't come to any agreement as to who should say her name first. Finally the old man compromised. "Say the first two letters."

Gurov told him, "*R-O.*"

Red Beard was terribly glad. He said, "You must work in the commandant's office."

"I do," Gurov replied.

He grabbed Ivan Tarasovich's hand, slapped him across the shoulder, and almost kissed him. "Oh," he exclaimed, "what luck! I know you're looking for the girl. I've been wanting to tell you about her being in our village for a long time now, but the men wouldn't let me go. You could say they arrested me. I couldn't manage to run away till just now. When I saw you, I thought you were involved in this business. I'm the *starosta* here—Afonkin. Perhaps you've heard of me?"

"I've heard," Gurov answered. "How fortunate that I met you!"

What shall I do? Ivan Tarasovich thought to himself. If I let him go, he'll inform the commandant and there'll be trouble. But how can I hold him back? Of course, he's an old man, but I have only one arm. I didn't take a weapon with me, because I was afraid of bumping into a search party.

Finally Gurov said, "You know what? You wait an hour or two for me here, Afonkin, while I go to the village. On the way back, I'll take you with me and present you to the commandant myself. I guarantee they won't begrudge you a reward."

Matters were arranged. Afonkin told Gurov who the children were living with, and Ivan Tarasovich left.

I'll show the feldsher Solomin's letter, the one-armed man thought. I'll ask him to prepare the children so they won't be afraid of me.

When Gurov got there, the trail was already cold. Another failure.

As Ivan Tarasovich told his story, guns boomed constantly. Machine guns *rat-a-tat-tated*. An explosion resounded, and firing could be heard through the thick, wooden shutters.

"Oh," exclaimed the old woman, "it seems close!"

"The devil!" Vasily Georgiyevich jumped up. "I can't sit still. Think of it. The last night of occupation! Maybe tomorrow morning it will be all over and life will begin again."

"In my detachment we tried not to talk about it," Gurov said. "You had to work and do your job, or you'd go out of your mind with impatience."

"True enough," answered the feldsher. "What happened next?"

"Well, it was like this. I showed Solomin's letter to Vladik, and we decided to come here. At the same time, I told our men where Afonkin was waiting. They went with me to meet him. I don't think things went too well for him. Vladik and I left at once. Evidently we walked much faster than you, because you weren't here when we arrived. I wondered whether or not something else had gone wrong, but here you are finally. . . ."

It became silent. Everyone was automatically listening to what was happening in the street. Shouts resounded through the shutters. They could hear people talking and running past their window.

"Good Lord," said Konushkin. "You know, I don't believe it! I can't imagine that I'll go out on the street tomorrow and live in my own home without having to fear anyone, mind you! Can you imagine that, Vasily Georgiyevich?"

Someone banged on the door. Everyone jumped.

"Stay calm!" said Gurov. "Now we'll find out

what has happened." He went into the corridor without hurrying.

The old woman, the feldsher, Konushkin, and the children stood listening.

"Who's there?" asked Ivan Tarasovich.

"Open up!" a voice answered. "Open up right now!"

"People are sleeping here," Gurov said persuasively. "You'll disturb them. Come back in the morning. Then we'll talk."

The person banged on the door again, this time with a gun butt. The bolt jumped and the door shook.

"Open up! Open up!" the voice demanded again. "I'll blow you out with a grenade."

Gurov looked back questioningly.

The feldsher and Konushkin shook their heads *no*.

"Right you are!" said Gurov. "If we have to die, we might as well go to the tune of music." He shouted, "Come back in the morning. Then we'll be happy to let you in, but right now it's impossible."

Vasily Georgiyevich took out his famous Mauser. There was an explosion somewhere nearby. Everyone involuntarily lowered his head.

Tanks were thundering down the road. Machine guns opened fire and continued without stopping. More people ran down the street. A small antiaircraft gun kept firing. Planes flew over the house. When the powerful, deafening roar of their motors stopped, everyone noticed that things became much quieter. The antiaircraft gun wasn't shooting anymore, and the machine guns were firing somewhere far in the distance.

Again there was a knock at the door.

"Well, aren't you going to throw the grenade?" Gurov asked politely.

"If anyone is in there, get out!" was heard from behind the door. "We've freed your God-forsaken little town, of course."

Gurov and Vasily Georgiyevich dashed to the door. Their hands sprang to the bolt, but it refused to obey. Despite their hindering of each other, they finally managed to draw it back.

The door opened wide. Early morning sunshine burst into the cellar. The bright light made everyone blink. A Soviet soldier, his face blackened with dust and his lips cracked and parched, stood in the doorway.

Just then the little boy who had been asleep in the

cellar woke up and went into the corridor. Seeing that nobody was paying any attention to him, he pulled at his grandmother's dress.

"Grandma," he said. "I'm up. I want to get dressed. It's time now."

"Yes, it's time," the old woman replied. "The time has come!" And she burst into tears.

25

Lena! Lena!

The next day a little boy and girl, holding hands, walked toward the ten-year school, which served as general headquarters. Officers were standing at the entrance to the building, smoking and chatting while waiting to be called into headquarters.

Going up to one of them, the boy said, "Comrade Commander, I must see General Rogachov."

Squinting, the officer looked at him. "What is your business, please?" he asked with extreme politeness, although the corners of his eyes crinkled and he seemed to be having difficulty holding back a smile.

"It's personal," the boy answered briefly and with dignity.

"Ah, personal!" replied the officer. The other soldiers standing around looked at one another and burst out laughing. "That's interesting. Why is it that all citizens your age or a little younger always must see General Rogachov and always on personal business?"

"I don't know."

"I'm going to give you some good advice, young comrade. Go to that building on the corner. The Political Section is located there. They can undoubtedly explain to you that a young man your age can be of use to his homeland without signing up as a volunteer in the Army."

The officers standing around roared with laughter. Kolya blushed and looked at Lena helplessly. She answered him with an equally helpless look. They went away and sat on the porch steps of the house next door.

They had to think hard about what to do next. Vasily Georgiyevich and Gurov, confident that Kolya and Lena would have no more trouble finding Rogachov, had decided not to accompany the children. They did not want to appear to be seeking the general's gratitude. Kolya understood the reasoning of these modest men. Now the children were on their own. Lena was very nervous and excited. She couldn't think of anything. No ideas came to Kolya's mind either.

A car approached the entrance. A short, gray general got out and went into headquarters. Officers stood at attention and saluted. The street became quiet again. Only the very distant boom of artillery fire could be heard. Far, far away Soviet units were continuing to advance.

Kolya was ravenous. He had been certain he'd be able to find General Rogachov right away and that the general would probably feed him dinner before sending him back to Grandfather. He had been so excited he had hardly eaten that morning. He hadn't taken anything from Vasily Georgiyevich's supplies. Besides he was very disappointed that after all his adventures they didn't even want to talk seriously with him. Lena kept looking at him with pleading eyes. She believed he could solve everything and fix anything.

Kolya was quite put out. Why did everyone count on him so much? He couldn't think of everything for all of them!

He began muttering in a low voice. "Well, if they won't let us in, they won't! I can't do a thing about it. I did what I could. Now I can't do anything else. I can't, and that's all there is to it."

Even without turning, he felt Lena's sad, helpless gaze on him. He got up and took her by the hand. "Come on, let's try again."

This time different officers were standing around headquarters. But when Kolya said he had to see Rogachov, they grinned just as the others had done.

This group of officers advised him to go to the Town Soviet, which had probably already begun to organize, instead of the Political Section.

Kolya decided not to back down. "My business is this," he said. "This girl is General Rogachov's daughter. Now do what you want. What's it to me? I'll leave if you like."

One of the officers who had turned away, having considered the conversation finished, returned in short order. "What's that?" he asked. "What did you say?"

"I told you," Kolya growled gloomily, "that this is the daughter of General Rogachov. That's our business. If you don't want to let us in to see him, you don't have to. I'll leave if you like."

Two more officers came over and began to listen. "Comrade Major," one of them said, "maybe it's really true! I've heard that the General's family was in occupied territory."

The major turned around to say something to the sentry, but at that moment the general came out of headquarters.

Kolya knew who he was right away. He sensed it from the strained effort with which the officers stood at attention and saluted. And he sensed it from the way Lena's hand shook in his own.

Rogachov was a tall, stately man in a general's uniform with three big stars on his shoulder straps. Gray temples peeked out from under his cap. He saluted the officers politely and started walking toward his car.

Kolya made up his mind. "Comrade General!" he shouted in an unexpectedly high-pitched little boy's voice. Dragging Lena along behind him, he ran up to Rogachov.

The general turned and gave him an intent, serious look.

"Comrade General," Kolya repeated, gasping for breath and on the verge of tears, "I . . . we . . . Grandfather told us to find you."

Rogachov looked past him. His eyes got big and round with astonishment. "Lena!" the general said. "Lena! Lena!" he repeated.

Lena was standing with her mouth wide open, unable to say a word. Tears were streaming down her face, and her lips were quivering. The general lowered his head and immediately became much shorter. Kolya noticed that Rogachov's lips were trembling, too. The general wanted to say something, but couldn't. He took a step forward and scooped Lena up in his arms. After turning around, he quickly took her into headquarters.

The last thing Kolya saw was Lena's tearstained face resting on her father's broad shoulders.

The officers were silent. Then one of them said, "Yes, comrades, that's the way things are!"

Kolya let the officers know how he felt about everything they had done. "Go to the Town Soviet!" he mimicked. "Go to the Town Soviet! You can have your old Town Soviet!" Turning his back on them, he went off down the street.

Once he had disappeared around the corner, a captain started after him, puffing and panting. Kolya could hear his shouts and footsteps perfectly well. "Little boy! Little boy!"

In the first place, Kolya considered his job done. Now he had to get home to Grandfather as quickly as possible. There was nothing for him to do here. He had his own affairs to look after. In the second place, he thought it was high time they stopped calling him "little boy."

The captain evidently understood his mistake himself. He saluted very politely and said, "General Rogachov requests your presence."

Kolya didn't answer. He was very excited. He even had a lump in his throat, and it was hard to speak. He turned and followed the captain.

The general met him in the doorway of his office.

He embraced him and kissed him three times, as is customary between Russian men.

With a tearstained face, Lena was sitting in an armchair, so happy that she could not utter a single intelligible word. General Rogachov was called to the telephone. They were left alone. Lena couldn't calm down and kept sobbing. Kolya, taking advantage of the general's absence, cried a little, too.

Then a major wrote down the names of Grandfather, the feldsher, and all the others, as Kolya dictated them. The boy explained that Grandfather and Aleksandra Petrovna were very far away, but the major only grinned and said it wasn't all that far.

They stayed overnight in headquarters. General Rogachov didn't want Lena to spend the night anywhere else. While dropping off to sleep, they watched the general's face, lighted by lamplight, bowed over his desk. They listened to his quiet, confident voice.

Grandfather woke the children in the morning.

During the night, they had brought everyone to headquarters—Solomin, Aleksandra Petrovna, and even the raven. Later on Gurov, Vasily Georgiyevich, Vladik, and Zhuk came. Last, but not least, came Lyosha and Niusha, who had been difficult to find. Lyosha was very embarrassed and loudly cleared his throat from time to time in hopes of showing he was at ease.

Niusha conducted herself with confidence. She shook everyone's hand and said, "Pleathed to meet you!"

They all ate dinner together and recalled past experiences and adventures. General Rogachov asked for the details and was very excited.

Ivan Ignatyevich told him how Lena's mother had died.

The general listened, pacing back and forth on his office floor. He stood with his back to them, silently looking out the window, for quite a while.

Then he spoke about the future. Of course, Solomin would return to Zapolsk, and Lena could go on living with him for the present.

Solomin was very happy. Life would have been boring for him without Lena. And the children didn't want to be separated.

Solomin invited Vladik to make his home with him, then began to persuade the feldsher and Aleksandra Petrovna to move to Zapolsk.

They decided against it. They had sick patients who couldn't be abandoned, and they were accustomed to their little village. But Vasily Georgiyevich agreed to let Vladik stay in Zapolsk and promised to come see him every month.

They decided that Ivan Ignatyevich Solomin and Kolya would move to Moscow with Rogachov after the war.

"Lena has been lucky," said Rogachov. "She has found a good grandfather and cousin, and she mustn't lose them."

After dinner they sat around for a long time dreaming about the end of the war and their future life in Moscow. They thought about how Vladik would enter the Medical Institute and how on Sundays they would go to the theater or the Park of Culture and Rest.

Zhuk jumped around the table. The raven, cocking its head to the side, screamed, "Raven! Little raven! Raven! Little raven!"

Glossary

balalaika—triangular three-stringed folk instrument, similar to a guitar or mandolin.

cupping glass—Hot cupping glasses are applied to the surface of a patient's skin to draw blood.

feldsher—an assistant doctor with limited academic training.

kasha—porridge made of oats, wheat, or buckwheat, that has been a Russian staple for many years.

kilometer—One kilometer is approximately ⅝ of a mile.

pood—Five poods are approximately 180 pounds.

samovar—Russian teapot.

selo—large village with government office building, where local administrative authorities are housed.

sheatfish—European species of catfish.

starosta—village elder who presides over local meetings and is official head of village.

ten-year school—In the Soviet school system, there are 8-year and 10-year schools. In time, the Soviets plan to have only 10-year schools.

verst—One verst is approximately ⅔ of a mile.

ABOUT THE AUTHOR

Yevgeny Samoilovich Ryss was born in 1908 and died in 1973. His first book was published in 1928, and he became a member of the Union of Soviet Writers in 1934. During his career he wrote ten books and twelve plays, most of them for children. The present book, first published in 1946, was made into a prize-winning film. As a reporter and war correspondent in World War II, Mr. Ryss undoubtedly witnessed many events similar to those described in this novel. His last published work, *Peter and Peter,* came out in the spring of 1973. The author's widow, Ludmila Ryss, lives in Moscow, U.S.S.R.

ABOUT THE TRANSLATOR

A native of Concord, New Hampshire, Bonnie Carey was awarded her B.A. in Slavic Languages and Literature from Boston University, summa cum laude, Phi Beta Kappa. Later she received her M.A. from Assumption College, Worcester, Massachusetts, and she is presently enrolled in a Ph.D. program at the University of North Carolina. A translator, poet, and teacher, Mrs. Carey is at present an instructor in Russian at the George B.S. Hale High School in Raleigh, North Carolina, where she makes her home.

Her husband, John J. Carey, is an electronic design engineer, and they have a son and a daughter.